SAVAGE GIRL

FAÎTE FALLING
BOOK TEN

MARY E. TWOMEY

Savage Girl

Book Ten in the Faîte Falling Series

By

Mary E. Twomey

COPYRIGHT

Copyright © 2017 Tuesday Androsian
Cover Art by Emcat Designs

All rights reserved.
First Edition: July 2017

For information:
http://www.maryetwomey.com

DEDICATION

For my Aunt Jeanne

Who is always a friend first.

SEVEN TEARS

When Dub told me he was taking me to the lowest level of my ring that held the deepest twisted magic, I guess I'd undersold just how jacked-up Faîte could get. "Whoa. You were right to close the ring and keep all of this locked inside. Dother and Dian really wanted to set all of this loose?"

"Now you understand why I prefer solitude to a world where my younger brothers roam free."

Despite our earlier fight, in which I'd punched Dub for keeping me a blind Vampire, and he'd slapped me across the face because, well, he's a jackhole, we put our differences aside in light of our grander mission. He kept one arm locked around my back, ensuring nothing snapped at me. While I could see now, I suddenly wished for the blessing that was blindness.

I tried not to whine like a baby, but the noise of distress

was crashing up against the inside of my lips. We walked carefully along a narrow path that was lined with crimson mud. The pasty, goopy redness radiated heat that made me sweat without getting within even a foot of the stuff. It bubbled like a cauldron's juices, and when the bubbles popped, a tiny scream erupted from the murky underground. On either side of the trail were what looked like termite hills, stretching at least five stories up into the orange sky. The glow from above highlighted the more disgusting features of our walk, letting me see softball-sized spiders, shiny cockroaches the size of birds, and silverfish as large as snakes skittering over the termite mounds. The sulfur smell didn't seem to bother them, but it made me bury my nose in the shoulder of Dub's black cloak.

It wasn't just the sight, but the sounds of moaning and wailing that echoed around us, seeming to come from everywhere and yet no place in particular. The heart-wrenching cries spoke of far too much torture – whether physical or emotional, I couldn't tell. Either way, my heart felt like it might start bleeding all over the place if I heard just one tale of woe that drove a person to cry out like that.

Worst was that I couldn't see them. Even with my sight back, I couldn't make out much beyond a yard or two out from our path. A smoky haze clung to the air, peppering the firmament with black, gray and swirls of maroon dust to obscure the faces of the damned.

"Try not to touch the bugs. Not a single brush of your toe," Uncle Dub warned me.

I shuddered, wishing I could get the sound of their slimy little bug legs out of my mind. It reminded me of thousands of people chewing with their mouths open, which I would've preferred to this. I like to think I've survived a fair amount of awfulness in my time with Avalon, but this was a new level of get-me-the-crap-out-of-here. I clung to Dub, despite my earlier anger at him. "I'm starting to forget why we're down here. Remind me why this is worth it?"

"We're looking for a Kelpie. Not just any old nag, but a specific one. Tell me, are you an emotional crier, or do you cry more easily at physical pain?"

"Huh?"

"Never mind. Perhaps we'll find him without any urging." He led us through the termite mound maze to a tranquil lake that had a faint orange mist hovering a foot above the glassy surface. "Do you hear any voices?"

I quirked my eyebrow at him. "You mean, other than the wailing and moaning?"

"Yes, there will always be that on this level. Do you hear any voices calling out to you with words you can understand?"

I craned my ear, hoping the absence of my sight in my normal life had granted me a heightened sense of hearing to rival a superhero. "I don't think so, but I'll keep an ear out."

He clicked his fingers a few times, but nothing happened to disrupt the waters as we walked the perimeter. "I can hear a great many things through your ring – things not even you hear, because they're said while you're sleeping. Such a waste, sleep." He kept his arm tight around my shoulders, securing me to his side in a gesture of protection, not affection, which was fine by me. He angled me away from the lake, peering out across the surface for... I'm not sure, but it seemed as if this whole place unnerved him. I guessed that if something put an ultra-powerful immortal on edge, I should probably stand down on whatever Lochness-Yeti-Abominable monster this was.

His eyes stayed trained on the water as he spoke to me. "This seems as good a place as any for a confession." He turned me to stand in front of him, squaring his shoulders to me with a stern expression. "One of the times you were sleeping, I heard Kerdik and Bastien talking. Bastien confessed a great many things to Kerdik on pain of much torture, which my nephew is quite good at. Bastien admitted to cheating on you, sleeping with another woman."

I stiffened, but breathed in a long drag of air that stank like rotting egg salad. Would that anything could purify the bile that rose up in me when I thought back on that dark period of our relationship. "I already knew about that. That was ages ago, way back in Avalon: Part One. We weren't married, and I found out about the whole thing. We've moved past it."

Dub's words came out slowly, delivering a punch to rival The Hulk. "This was shortly after you returned from your honeymoon. The woman he slept with got pregnant, and she gave birth to a son. Apparently, the boy looks just like his father. Bastien sneaks away while you're sleeping sometimes to go visit his other family."

It was like a bowling ball that kept crashing into pins, making a wreck of what was supposed to be a perfect order of things. My feet stopped moving as my brain skipped over what I'd assumed was real and true. "No," I insisted, my eyebrows furrowed. "You're wrong. Whatever you thought you heard, that's not true. Bastien wouldn't step out on me."

"Again," Dub reminded me. "Step out on you *again*, you mean. Kerdik suspected foul play because there were a few jewels missing from one of your family's safes. Bastien's been using your inheritance to pay for Bastien II's life. That's his son's name."

It was like being walloped in the stomach by someone who doesn't have an accurate barometer to measure pain. Only one note rang above all the others. "Bastien II? The little boy is named after him?"

"I suppose if you two ever have a son someday, Bastien III is still open. Or perhaps you can name him Bastien II, just like his half-brother. That might create a bit of competition, though."

"You're wrong!" I yelled, though Dub hadn't raised his voice through the whole explanation. "You're wrong, and I'll prove it to you. Bastien would never cheat on me while we're married. When I wake up and get back home, I want you to press your ear to the clouds so you can hear him tell me that he didn't..." My breath came in shallow pants, and I worried that my heart might up and die in my chest with no fanfare.

"Lane should've told you, I always thought. She was worried he might leave you if there was a confrontation, and she would be stuck with Kerdik for a son-in-law." He stopped at the shore and helped me to sit on the sand. The granules appeared almost reddish when they sifted around our movements.

I shook my head, piecing together Dub's words in an order that made me choke on my worst fear. I pulled my knees to my chest and stared out at the water. "You're wrong. My husband loves me, and Lane would've told me."

Dub watched my face, and then let out a long sigh. "Oh, fine. I made the whole thing up to get you to cry."

I turned to balk at him. "What? Do you not have enough drama in your life? Are you hoping to catch yourself a beating?"

"No, I was hoping to make you cry. It's the easiest way to summon him in a pinch."

"Summon who? The medic you're going to need after you choke on my fist? That was low, Dub. Seriously. I can't believe you'd throw my relationship under the bus just so you could phone a friend." I stood, angry and wondering how I kept trusting him, if this was all it ever got me.

"Rosie, wait. It's the best way to summon a Kelpie. They feed off of tears, so if you shed seven tears into a lake where one lives, they'll come to the surface for more."

I threw my arms out when he followed after me – not like I had any idea where I was going. "All you ever do is tell me riddles, old man. I'm tired of you, and all of this. We're supposed to be finding a way to get a message to Kerdik, not making me question one of the few solid truths in my life. Man, I can't believe I fell for it again! I keep thinking you're this good guy underneath the emotional poison your family must've been growing up, but you prove me wrong at every turn."

"Stop right now, or I'll intervene. I'm certain you don't want that." His voice had the firmness of a command to it, but I ignored him, stomping away from the source of a hefty portion of frustration in my life.

"Ah!" I cried out when I was struck with sudden blindness. I made it four more steps before I tripped over what was probably just an uneven clump of sand. I pitched forward, catching myself on the warm embankment, heaving my anger on all fours like a savage beast. "Leave me alone!" I snapped as his hands found my shoulders. "You're as selfish as they come. This is my life, Dub! Don't you get that? This is my life, and you're stepping all over me whenever it serves your greater purpose. Don't you know that the world already does that without any encouragement from you?"

"Rosie, I…"

"No! I'm tired of you always jerking me around, like I'm some big joke. My marriage isn't a joke! My sight isn't a joke, either! I'm a person, which is something I shouldn't have to say to my own uncle!" My eyes burned with unshed tears, and I despised that, of all things, I was crying in front of someone so heartless.

Dub guided me to the water's edge, kneeling next to me and rubbing soothing circles into my back. "You sacrifice so much for a world that's not even yours."

I don't know why this made the tears flow more freely. "Why can't I have a regular life? I loved Wednesday night bowling, and Thursday indoor soccer matches. I loved playing with Lucas and debating with Lane where I should do my veterinary internship. Lucas probably won't even remember who I am by the time I get back! Don't you care how that feels?"

"I'm sure it'll be a short period of reacquainting yourselves, and then you'll be his favorite aunt in no time."

I swatted at him angrily. "Don't be nice to me! I don't need you to be insincere when I'm having a moment."

"I don't like to see you so upset, little flower. I didn't mean to cause you this much pain."

"This is exactly what you meant to do! Bastien's one of the few people in my life I can trust to always have my back, and you made me question that. Then bringing Lane into the lie? Lane is precious to me! You don't have anyone who's precious to you, so you crap all over my life, like it's all no big deal."

Dub waited a few beats before placing his hand on my back again. "You don't like what the soldiers did to her."

I flinched at the thing I tried never to think about, because Lane had asked me to deal with it that way. She didn't want me to see her bloody, beaten, naked and tied to a post. She wanted me to see her as a strong, smart and confident woman who was capable of anything. I tried my best to erase the memory that had burned itself into the innermost crevices of my bruised psyche.

My chest tightened over the agony that I hadn't been able to rescue her. Feeling the pain and desperation of someone you love hits far harder than the sting of your own sufferings. "If there was one person who deserves a good life without a single ounce of that garbage, it's her. How could they..." I gulped, feeling the tears dripping off my nose. I let out a gut-twisting cry that echoed across the surface of the water. "She's my mother!"

Dub's arms encircled me, leaning me to his chest so he could run his fingers through my hair. "That's more than enough tears, now. Close your eyes, so you're not over-whelmed when I give you your sight back."

I obeyed, wishing I had anyone else in the world to offer me a little bit of comfort right about now. "I miss my mom," I admitted, knowing I probably should've stopped needing her so badly by now. But some part of me knew that no matter how grown I got, I would always find my way back to the woman who taught me to be strong, smart and capable of just about anything. It was her teachings in me that rose up when opposition threatened too much of what I loved. It was her voice that belted out of me when injustice arose that didn't need to be. My words rang in my ears as the rest of my tears soaked into Dub's shirt. The lake filled my vision when I opened my eyes, but the cry of my heart was still a resounding, "I need my mom!"

"I know you do," he said with real gentleness in his voice. "I shouldn't have made you question Bastien. After everything he's been through, he's remained loyal. I'm sure others would've walked away, knowing Kerdik was so very tied to you, but he's never looked back on the life he could've had without you by his side. Not that I can tell, anyway."

"I don't need you to comfort me after you just smashed me to pieces."

Dub watched the lake while he spoke to me. "My kindness often comes across as cruel. Right now, you're mad I invoked real sadness in you, but there's a greater danger you must stay focused on. Dother and Dian have your body, Rosie." He paused so we could both ponder the very real fear that gripped us.

Dian (Kerdik's uncle), and Dother (Kerdik's father – I only remember which one is which because "Dother" rhymes with "father") were living up to the hype that accompanied big, bad villains. They kidnapped my body after I'd taken too much mayapple root so I could heal the rest of the *Farouche* Vampires in Avalon. They wanted to lure Kerdik into a trap, and I was pretty sure it would work. It was a waiting game now, and asleep as my body was, there was nothing I could do to fight back.

Dub squeezed my arm to center me. "Dian and Dother have no forethought unless it concerns their master plan – and there is no small evil in his dreams for a better Faîte. Hate me if you must, but I'm trying to save you right now."

"By making me cry?"

"Yes," he answered without hesitation.

"Why didn't you just make yourself cry, instead of poking at my life?"

He let out a superior "pfft" but didn't otherwise answer. "Seven tears should've done it. Where is he?"

As if waiting for dramatic effect, the waters began to ripple, the tiny splashes turning into three-foot-tall waves within seconds. I gripped Dub's black shirt, disoriented at going from total blindness to a live-action ocean movie at my fingertips. "Whatever you do, don't touch the Kelpie."

"What's a Kelpie?"

My question was moot, because it was in the very next breath that the surface of the water parted, ripping a gasp straight from my lungs.

2

PERVY SEIRBIGH

I thought I was pretty much awe-proof after all Faîte had shown me. But as the Kelpie's head parted the water, my jaw was in permanent holy-crap-mode. "Whoa. He's huge!" The black horse with a slick coat was easily the size of a small elephant, seeming to unfold from the lake like a just-add-water toy that expanded beyond control.

"Don't touch him," Dub reminded me, pulling me to my feet. The desire to back up was strong, but Dub held me to his side, standing his ground with some measure of defiance you had to respect. "Seirbigh, I was hoping you'd come."

The horse was dark, big, and glared at us with black eyes that were filled with malice I knew I hadn't earned. He scrutinized us in a way that was almost human. His mane consisted of two-inch thick ropes of long... seaweed?

I expected him to respond with the unspoken animal language, but his maw opened to let out audible words, like Mr. Ed himself. "Whose tears tasted so very sweet? Was it ye, Dub? Did ye finally look back on your long life and see how worthless ye are?"

Dub's eyes darted skyward in exasperation. "It was the Avalon Rose. I told you about her last year, remember? The Vampire girl who was born to Morgan le Fae and King Urien?"

Seirbigh's enormous eyes zoomed in on me, studying me to see if I measured up to the fairytales Dub had told him about me. My mouth was too dry to speak, so I let him stare at me, calculating my every move – miniscule as they were. It wasn't that he was a large fella, it was the pure malice in his eyes that turned me into an introvert. I clung to Dub's shirt even tighter, gripping without any thought of letting go.

Seirbigh licked his lips before they curved into a malicious grin. "Rosalie of Avalon, eh? Ye can interrupt my solitude anytime." He drew out the next sentence, milking it for all it was worth. "Your sadness is delicious."

I blanched at the borderline sexual way he spoke to me. I still didn't speak, but snaked my arm around Dub's waist, in case he got any bright ideas about tossing me into the lake and feeding me to the Kelpie. "Rosie will be my niece," Dub declared, holding me tight to his chest. "She's promised to my nephew, Kerdik."

"Ye fancy a green fellow?" Seirbigh snorted derisively

from his spot a few yards away in the lake. "Must be an arranged marriage. Kerdik could never catch a beauty like tha without contract or mind-melding magic."

"I love Kerdik," I spouted back, finally finding my voice.

"So she speaks, does she? And what does she have to say to me? She summons me but doesn't seem to need anything. They always need something." Then I heard his thoughts trailing off when his mouth stopped moving. *"If I was in my man form, the things I could do to her. If her tears are tha sweet, I'll bet she tastes even better when..."*

"Hey, that's enough outta you. Be pervy on your own time." When Seirbigh's eyes widened, I scowled up at him. "That's right, I can hear you being disgusting. Clean it up for the viewers, pal."

"I didn't say anything."

"I can hear your thoughts." When that didn't ring any bells, I wondered just how long he'd been cooped up inside the ring. "Kerdik gave me a blessing when I was born, letting me hear unknown languages. I can hear the thoughts of animals, so keep yours PG, if you don't mind."

Just like that, Seirbigh went from being an insufferable tool to splashing in the lake like an overjoyed puppy. "I've never heard of magic so grand! Kerdik did tha, did he? Well, I'll bet tha steamed the Sons of Carman right good. They can never manage to hold onto blessings long enough to deliver them." As he neared, I expected him to tower over us, but he seemed to be shrinking in conjunction with his excitement. By the time he reached the shore, he was the size of a normal horse, if not a little smaller. He grinned at me, and then shot Dub a superior glance. "I'll bet tha's why ye never mentioned the birth blessing to me. Ye didn't want any of us down here to know the black sheep of the family surpassed ye. Kerdik can wrangle a blessing like tha?" He shook his head at Dub, in utter glee at what he presumed would be Dub's total humiliation. "Tha must've made ye burn with jealousy."

Dub's nose rose in the air. "I'm only ever proud of Kerdik. He's accomplished much, and perhaps it was because he was so separate from us that he went on to do all he has. He created Avalon on his own; it's no great surprise that he has learned nuances of magic that've been hidden from me while I've been cooped up in here."

When it was clear Dub couldn't be goaded, Seirbigh inclined his head to me. *Ye can hear me right now?*

My shoulders lifted slightly. "Of course. Are there others of you in the lake, or are you the only one?"

"There are others, but I'm the master of the Kelpies. I get first pick of anyone who nears the lake." He looked at me and licked his overlarge lips.

I grimaced. "Dude, gross."

Dub took control of the conversation, which was good, since Seirbigh seemed like a total tool (even though his seaweed mane was pretty cool). "We're only here because we require your help. Rosie's in this place because she wears the ring we were all trapped in. Kerdik entrusted it to her, and it's because of her care that we're still alive in here."

I quirked my eyebrow at Dub, but said nothing. I wasn't the reason they were all alive. All I did was not take the stupid ring off, which was no grand feat.

Dub pressed on. "Her body's in danger. When Dother and Dian escaped, they didn't waste any time forming a plan."

"Let me guess, the Vampires and the Werewolves are running wild?" Seirbigh sounded bored at the prediction that was spot on. "Oh, the good old Brothers of Destruction, always living up to their name."

"Indeed. Rosie's been curing them, which is why we've seen an influx of Vampire magic returned to the ring."

Seirbigh let out a contemptible snort. "It's your job to keep track of the magic; I just watch the lake. She's been sending Vampire magic back in here? Fine. Tha doesn't concern me. Faîte doesn't concern me."

"It should. If Dother and Dian run amok out there, they'll crack open the ring, and all the creatures will spill out."

"Then let it come! Let us out of here!" Seirbigh whinnied.

"How about we just let *you* out of here?" Dub tempted him, quietly dangling the carrot to get the desired results. "If you find Kerdik and deliver a message, Rosie will grant you, and only you, your freedom. The rest of the Kelpies will remain locked in here. How would you fancy being the only Kelpie in Faîte? You'd have your pick of any of the lakes, and could remain out of sight for as long as you like. You could take victim after victim down with you before anyone puts the pieces together."

When Dub's smile turned sinister, I backed away from the two. I was wary of the agreement I didn't understand, and that didn't sound all that safe for the world at large.

There was a moment's pause, in which I listened to Seirbigh consider Dub's offer, weighing the cons with the very big pros before he spoke. "All I have to do is find Kerdik and give him a message?"

Dub nodded. "That's all. Then you're free to roam Faîte at will. The only Kelpie in the world."

Seirbigh postured with a fool's pride. "Aye. I'll do it, then."

I began to flick through the holes in this plan. I couldn't get him out of this place. It had been a complete fluke before when the magic had spilled out. Dub tucked me back into his side as he motioned for Seirbigh to follow. "Come. I'll write the note, and you'll be off on your adventure."

Judging by Dub's taut abdomen and the strained muscles in his neck, things weren't as foolproof as he needed us to believe.

3

THERE'S NO SUCH THING AS FREE BREAD

We'd made our way up one level, away from the skeeviest magic layer, but not to our meadow just yet. Apparently, this was as high as Seirbigh could make it, due to the wards the Brothers of Destruction had set in place to keep the riffraff out. It was gray, craggy rock here, with cold pockets of air passing through us like apparitions. I didn't trust Dub, but in this land of Dante's imagination, I didn't stray from his side.

"Stay here," Dub instructed the leering horse. "We'll fashion the note, and then you'll be off." Dub didn't wait for Seirbigh's response, but kept climbing skyward, up the rickety ladder, whose rungs were covered in what looked like dried, yet still somehow goopy, sheep's skin.

I slipped twice, trying not to be worried about the wispy ghost-like masses that swirled around, whipping by us but never touching down. "Dub? What are these things?"

"Oh, just the *Farouche* Vampire magic," he said without concern. "The white puffs are Vampires, and the brown ones are Werewolves."

I clung to the slippery ladder. "Are you serious? Are they going to infect us? Shouldn't we be... I dunno, not here?"

"This is the level I've dedicated to trapping the lost magic on. It's out of the way enough so that it doesn't bother me on a daily basis. Not to worry. It won't hurt you. You're not real."

I scoffed. "Come again?"

"Your body is still in Faîte. The you that's in here is part of your mind, not your real body. The lost magic I'm trapping on this level is harmless. It needs live bodies to really make a dent."

I shivered as I climbed up the ladder behind Dub. It was easily the height of a four-story building, and stretched into the low-hanging clouds. The twilight atmosphere made the wisps easy to see, giving me the creeps when they brushed near my arms. "Hurry! I don't like it here."

Dub chuckled, because he's a jag. "You fear the innocuous? What a child you still are. I guess that'll distract you from the reality of torture you most certainly will undergo when your body wakes up. Fear that, little flower. Fear the Masters of All Things. That, I won't fault you for."

"I have half a mind to throw you off this ladder!" I stormed, pausing as he kicked out his leg from above me to make sure I didn't grab at him.

When we reached our regular level, I breathed in deep the scent of the meadow. The abstract shapes and colors that had once been were now beginning to look a little more like the trees and clouds they were when I wasn't drugged by the mayapple root. While it made for a lovely setting, worry lodged itself in my throat that I would be waking up soon.

"Wow, that's a boatload better than the rotting egg salad stink down there. I don't even mind the high-pitched ringing." The quiet but persistent sound was from my body being separated from my *lueur*, alerting me that Bastien was nowhere near.

"You get used to it." Dub snapped his fingers twice, and a scroll of parchment appeared, along with a quill and ink pot. Judah would've tripped out to see how cool the tip looked when Dub withdrew it from the pot and started writing. It was classic evil genius in action. "I'm telling Kerdik where you are, and what we heard from Dother."

"Cool. So, not for nothing, but I super don't know how to get a creature out of this ring. And isn't that kind of dangerous? Like, isn't the whole point of this place to make sure the nasty magic can't escape at random?"

"It is, and you don't need to worry about that. I can open the ring from here, just for a fraction of a minute, so hopefully only Seirbigh gets out. I can close it back up before anything else escapes."

I balked at Dub. "Are you serious? You've been able to get out any old time? How long have you known how to escape?"

He shrugged as he scrawled on the page. "Only a few years. I didn't think it worth mentioning to Dother and Dian. Their presence in Faîte has been nothing but a nuisance, so my judgment was prudent on that front. I like my domain here, and have no interest to see how far Faîte has fallen without us. Or worse, how much it thrived without our interference."

"Then why don't *you* just go, instead of sending that Kelpie dude? What sorts of victims were you two talking about back there? Are we unleashing something dangerous out of the ring? Because I don't want that."

"Kelpies are quite dangerous, yes. They find people who come near the water, and beckon them in. Once they touch the Kelpie, their hand sticks to him, and he takes them into the depths to drown them. Then he feasts on the body, and throws the entrails onto the shore."

I balked at Dub. "What? Gross! We can't let this dude back into Faîte if that's what he does in his spare time."

Dub waved off my concern with a flick of his wrist, as if I was being silly. "You don't need to worry about that. Seirbigh won't be alive for long. He'll deliver the message, which is the only thing that matters. I've included a line here for Kerdik to dispose of Seirbigh, once he's run his errand."

"Um, that seems pretty toolish, even for a vigilante mission. And won't Seirbigh just open up the scroll and read it?"

"It's in an old, long-forgotten language that Seirbigh wouldn't be able to decipher. Kerdik knows it, and that's the important part." He finished scribbling on the page, and then handed the quill to me.

My eyes went wide and my palms started to sweat. "Um, I can't actually… Could you jot it down for me?"

Dub threw his head back. "Of course. I forgot about your malady. What would you like me to say?"

My fingers twisted the hem of my shirt as my mind went completely blank. Of all the things I wanted to say, now that I had the chance, I couldn't think of a single one. I wanted to make sure Kerdik was okay, but that wasn't really a possibility. "I guess it would be counterintuitive to ask him to stay away from the danger, right?"

"Yes, very."

"I don't like that we're sending him into the lion's den."

"Yes, but we're sending him with a warning to watch out for the lions. I also put in here that Dian and Dother's ability to fly or levitate has been stripped. They can port, but that's all. Hopefully that might give him an edge." His eyes shot to me when I was quiet. "You're welcome for that, by the way. It's not easy to subtly strip an immortal of one of his basic abilities."

"You're the shiz," I offered without emotion. "We're asking Kerdik to fight his own father. His uncle. Is there anyone else who can do it?"

"No. Well, perhaps Brìghde or Cailleach, but from what I've heard of your conversations, neither of them have been able to be reached. I can jot something in there to give one more attempt to find them, use them as backup when he goes in. Then he'll have stronger numbers in the attack."

"Yeah, put that in for sure."

Dub snorted as he wrote. "Though, with all Dother and Dian are doing by sending out free bread to Éireland, I'm not sure the people will want Brìghde and Cailleach back."

The air felt like it stilled around me as something vital clicked in my brain. I reached out and gripped my uncle's shoulder, startling him with my stern squeeze. "Dub, wait! At the bar in Éireland, I overheard someone say that the Masters of All Things were instituting free bread for the masses. I thought it was part of the political campaign to win people over after they kind of stole the show from Queen Shavon, but what if it's more than that?"

He frowned, turning his head from the parchment to take in the worry on my face. "What do you mean?"

"I mean, have you ever known your brothers to be altruistic, and give away free food to the land they're about to rip apart? I wouldn't bother with that if I were them. They don't care about loyalty, or getting the kingdom to like them. Isn't it strange that they're trying so hard now?" I scolded myself for not putting this together sooner. "Do you think it's possible for them to put something wonky into that bread?" My hands gripped his forearms tight as my mind caught up with the itch my subconscious had been working on. "The Vampire and Werewolf curse! This is how they'll test out the population, weeding out the ones who turn, and keeping close the ones who don't so they can rebuild their new and improved Faîte! You said they wanted to destroy Faîte and start from scratch with the strongest and best. That's why no matter how hard I work to cure them, more and more Vamps keep popping up! It's not that it's airborne still, it's that they're making more Vamps to seek out the ones who are immune to the mutation!"

Dub's nostrils flared. "I don't know how that escaped my notice. I've been trying to listen in on everything I possibly can, but sometimes I duck out when things get too..."

I tried to guess how he was about to finish that sentence, but nothing came to mind. I wasn't doing anything weird in the bar when I'd overheard that. I was just sitting there by myself and drinking, occasionally chatting with Lugh or Molly. "Too boring?"

"I don't like feeling pity for you. Your blindness is sometimes a necessary limitation, and I'll not take that tool off the table completely before my brothers are out of the picture. There's no other way to motivate Kerdik, besides using you."

I reared back, shocked that Dub felt anything like remorse for his actions. "Wow. I guess you're not a one-dimensional bad guy after all. Good to know."

His long nose raised in the air, as if I'd insulted him. "I'm plenty bad, thank you very much. I just happen to take the time to see the big picture. Dother and Dian wish for Faîte to have a new hierarchy. Them at the top, of course."

"Obviously. That's Evil Megalomaniac 101."

"Right, you are. Then the purebloods under them, the Dullahan as their army, and the Vampires and Werewolves as their slaves. The lesser creatures would serve a purpose, as well. The Sluaghs would suck the souls from any opposition, and the Banshees would serve a slave-like purpose for the new kingdom. It was their grand plan when they were in here. I didn't realize they'd found a way to infect the people without them knowing. I thought the plan was still in the works." He touched his middle finger to the center of his forehead, squinching his eyes shut as he factored in this new information. He began writing with renewed purpose, finally turning back to me when he'd finished. "Did you have anything you wanted to say to my nephew before I seal this?"

"Kerdik has all the important information?"

"Of course. He'll be to your body in no time after reading this."

I swallowed my first two responses, landing on instructions, rather than my heart. "Please write that I would like him to bring a vial of Bastien's blood to tide me over, but to make sure Bastien stays safe, and away from it all. Especially that Kerdik keeps Bastien away from Dother and Dian." I pursed my lips, wishing there were better words than the obvious ones. "Tell Kerdik that I love him, no matter how it all shakes out. That if he can't save me, I understand." I shoved my hands in my jean pockets and addressed the grass. "If something happens to my body, I'd like him to check in on Lane from time to time, if it's not too much trouble."

"Is that all?"

I stared at the toe of my shoe, embarrassed. "You got the love stuff?"

"I did."

"Tell him, 'Your Uncle Dub is proud of you, and he's impressed with all you've learned to do.'"

He narrowed his eyes at me. "That's overstepping, young lady."

My mouth drew in a taut line. "I don't give a crap. You blinded me. I'll overstep if I feel like it."

Dub turned and scribbled something in haste. "Fine. Your impertinence is taxing, though. My nephew is going to need enough longsuffering to last him several lifetimes, if he's to be stuck with you."

I shot him half a smile at his snark, but it quickly fell away. "You really think this'll work?"

"My dear, I think it's the only thing that'll work."

4

SUCKING ON ROTTEN TUNA

Sending Seirbigh off was anticlimactic. The scroll was tied around his neck on the second level, Dub chanted a few unintelligible words, and Seirbigh was sucked out through a vacuum. Never thought I'd see a horse fly, but that was worth the carnival ticket's price of admission. It was like he'd been yanked from his spot in front of us, straight through the black mist and into Nowheresville. Or, more accurately, Faîte.

"You're certain my nephew is in Avalon? It would do us no good if we sent Seirbigh to the wrong continent."

I tapped my gut. "I'm sure. Hey, Dub? How long do you think I've been out?"

"Two days, perhaps?"

I nodded. "Am I going to start going crazy for Bastien in here? Like, does this place grant me some sort of Vampire immunity?"

"It doesn't. You'll feel the same pains, the same rabid thirst for your mate. I'm afraid I can't conjure up anything that might help, either."

I nodded, frowning as I banded my arms around my stomach. "It's cool."

I'd said "it's cool," but by day six, Dub confined me to a legit cage. I'd bitten him twice, even though his blood did nothing for me.

When I started gnawing on my own knuckles in the small cell he'd made me, he came in and carefully tied my arms behind my back. "I'm not going to hurt you," he cooed soothingly. "I'm only restraining you so you don't hurt yourself anymore. I can't stand to watch you cut yourself open just to drink your own blood. It's unsightly."

Instead of answering with some pithy retort, I simply snarled at him, my jaws snapping. I didn't mean to sound so venomous, and quickly quieted my acerbic angst to a more manageable level. I was without Bastien, which was bad for me in more than just the obvious way.

"Your husband's still got your *lueur*," Dub reminded me. We were on the highest level in our meadow, which emitted that incessant high-pitched ringing I swore I'd eventually get used to. "You're not going to feel like yourself until he's returned to you. The hunger is the worst part, I'm sure, but the missing *lueur* isn't helping matters."

Dub sat in the cell next to me, the grass beneath us tickling my nose as I lay on the ground like an animal. I felt like a beast, for sure – snorting through my pain as my limited options produced nothing of value.

"Make it stop!" I begged, hating how pitiful I sounded. When Dub's hand sifted through my hair, I craned my neck to bite him, even though I knew his blood wouldn't satisfy.

"Oh, go ahead. Take a drink. You'll see it's not me who can sustain you." He slid his hand from my hair to my face, letting me sink my fangs into his palm. It was the first bite that got my heart racing. The anticipation of relief hit me with the swing of a sledgehammer. My fangs sank into the meat of his hand, piercing easily to get at my meal. I didn't even have the sense to despise the person I'd become with all of this. I only saw the blood, only craved more and more of it.

I hated my plight even more when I swallowed something as foul as Dub. I choked down a few long swallows before I spat out the acrid taste of the man who was all wrong. It was only Bastien who tasted like food to me, and only him who could satiate. It was like being starved for food, but then being given rotting tuna as your only meal. You knew you wanted food, but the only thing on the plate made you want to vomit, and wasn't quite right for your body.

Dub's blood trickled down the side of my face as I cried out to the sky for someone or something to save me. "Bastien!" I shouted, as if that might call him nearer. My joints ached, and my bones felt like they were each being pressed in a vice. Every movement was agony, but I couldn't stop twisting from the hunger that was slowly driving me insane.

Dub wiped his hand off on his pants, and then went back to trying to calm me by playing with my curls. "Now, now. It won't always feel like this."

"Knock me out or something, Dub! I'm serious, I can't take this. Just let me sleep through it."

"If only it was that easy. I'm sorry, sweet girl. We'll get you back to your husband soon."

I was about to open my mouth to argue, but it was at that moment the sky seemed to open again, with a voice from the outside world. "Get her into the dungeon. It's Kerdik."

A second voice replied with venom dripping from his tone. "There's no time. Something tells me this won't be the father-son reunion he always hoped for as a boy. Blast him with everything you've got when he steps inside. Not before, though. We need him trapped."

Dub and I tensed, freezing all movement so we could hear the ensuing fight that would determine perhaps too much of Faîte.

5

FACING KERDIK'S DEMONS

*D*ub and I had surround sound seats to the fight of the century, but couldn't see what was happening. The scenery was still the field where we'd spend too many nights fighting, then finding a way back to coexisting, and then devolving back to bickering again. That seemed to be our way.

The two of us were silent, listening with rapt attention as the shouts of men filled the meadow. I assumed it was Kerdik, busting his way into the castle, instead of politely knocking. My guy had a certain charm about him that you kind of got used to.

At first there were no words, only explosions that shook my confidence and rattled my excruciatingly sore bones. Going this long without blood made everything hurt, but the pain was secondary to the fear that Kerdik was facing his abusive father for the first time in decades.

"Give her to me, Dian," Kerdik spat, making my heart rally. It was one thing to grow warm when a man told you he loved you, but it was an entirely other thing when that very same man faced his childhood and adulthood demons if there was a chance he could rescue you. I didn't like being helpless, but it was a relief to know that Kerdik would fight for me, regardless of how many monsters he would have to stand up against.

Another explosion boomed through the field, followed by Dian's higher-pitched laugh. "You finally figured it out that we have your little girlfriend. Very well, you can have her back, but the ring stays here."

"That's going to be a problem," came the voice of Cailleach. Her crone's cackle made me rally with relief that Kerdik was not alone. "Only Rosie can take it off, and I've warned her against it. Since she's as lifeless as they come right now, the ring will stay right where Kerdik put it."

"My dear Cailleach," Dother tutted, almost affectionate. His voice was low and deep. While Dian was snide in his demeanor, Dother was purely sinister when he spoke. "Don't you know we don't need mortals for things we can take care of ourselves?"

"Give her to us, or we'll tear your castle down, brick by brick!" It was Brìghde's voice that was shouting now, confirming that the good guys outnumbered the d-bags. I heard the walls begin to shake, and wanted to remind them that there were servants in their castle, no doubt, and they didn't deserve to die just because they'd been caught in the wrong place at the very wrong time.

"What a terrible threat. Tear down something that took us half a day to build? Tell me, do you intend to kick sand in our faces, too?" Yeah, Dian was a brat.

When the walls trembled and I heard a few things fall, Dother spoke up. "If you ruin our castle, you'll kill the few purebloods we've been gathering up. We only employ the best here."

"Of course you care about something as useless as blood purity," Kerdik snarled. "Leave it to Father of the Year to care deeply about a handful of subjects for all the wrong reasons."

Dother was quick with his retort. "You were never my son. I'll raise myself up a hundred sons who won't disappoint me at every turn. If only you were worth the pain you caused your mother. Kali would roll in her grave if she could see you now. A slave to your failing land, friends with mere mortals, and heartstrings tied to a woman you'll have to wait for. You're a king among insects, and yet you still ask for her permission." I heard him spit, and wanted to punch him in the face. "You turned out exactly as I expected – a complete and utter failure."

A thunk broke the tension, and Dian was not amused, his voice higher pitched than Dother's low, weighty timbre. "Is this some sort of joke? You sent an archer to shoot flaming arrows at us? How weak do you think we are, that you assume a flaming arrow could take us down?"

"Duck!" Kerdik shouted, and then a puff of something sounded, making Dother and Dian cry out in pain.

"Lugh," I informed Dub. "It must be Lugh, fighting for Kerdik from a far-off vantage point. He's Cross Shot. Never misses."

Dub's hand was gripping a chunk of my hair tightly. "I recall Cross Shot. Let's hope he lives up to his name today."

Someone must've charged, because there was a crash, and then several cries of intense physical strain. Dub cut my arms loose when he heard my whimpering. My bones hurt so badly; it was hard to move without feeling like my arms were being wrenched from the sockets. His arm banded around me after he sat me up, and his other hand held onto mine when I started gnawing at my fingers again, trying to bite myself to satiate my hunger.

I couldn't make heads or tails of the fight, which had quickly devolved into a battle. Dub was just as tense, and I knew he had a vested interest in both sides of the fray. His face twitched with each cry, no matter who it came from. "Grab her cane," Dub urged like a baseball fan sitting in the bleachers behind home plate. "Come on, Kerdik. Just take Cailleach's cane and finish it!"

"He won't do it," I reminded Dub. "Kerdik won't risk letting Carman out. You know that. Look what happened when Dother and Dian escaped. It's been pure chaos!"

"Kerdik wants this over with. He wants order restored to Faîte, and he knows this is the only way. He won't be able to contain Dother and Dian in the ring again. They're too powerful now. I don't see how it can be done." He squeezed my hand in a way that was supposed to be reassuring, but only made me cry out at the gentle pressure. "Apologies."

"Don't mention it."

"If Kerdik somehow does manage to do the impossible and trap my brothers in here once more, this will be our last conversation for a while. If they're stuffed back in here with me, remember that they might someday learn about this secret level I've built to be able to listen in on your life. Eventually they might be able to hear you, so keep my loyalties secret."

I leaned my head to his shoulder and nodded. "Of course. We'll have to come up with a code name for you."

Dub's humble confession came out almost bashfully. "I've always been partial to Theodore."

"Teddy, it is."

"Theodore," he corrected me with a squinty eye.

We both cringed when Kerdik cried out, "Don't touch her! Your fight's with me, Dian. Put her down!"

"You think your little trick's impossible to best, Callie, but it's not. You can have the girl, but I'll walk out of here with the ring!"

"Dian, put down the cleaver!" Kerdik commanded, his order laced with fear. "Rosie, wake up!"

I drew in a breath, and in the next second, let it out with a scream that would've made opera singers jealous.

Agony like I'd never known shot from my hand all the way through my body, and the next thing I knew, Theodore and the meadow were ripped from my vision.

6

MY FATHER-IN-LAW'S INFERNO

Being awoken to the sounds of your own screams is something no one should have to go through. While laid out on some sort of high stone table, I saw rubble of a castle in the process of being torn down, with sturdy two-foot long stone blocks being psychically thrown to the floor.

I blinked and saw two faces: one I didn't recognize, and one I very much did. "Make it stop!" I begged Kerdik, pleading with him for something to calm the excruciating agony that made it feel like my wrist was on fire. I writhed on the table, unable to make sense of which way was up when my mind was so twisted with torture. Tears started to cloud my vision, but not before my eyes drank their fill of Kerdik's terrified face. Oh, how I'd missed the sight of him.

"I can fix it!" He pleaded with me to believe him, but I didn't understand what he meant.

Before he could explain, Dother ripped Kerdik away from me. "What did you do to him? Dian, wake up, brother!"

Then they fell away from view, crashing through the debris. My body jerked on its own, my head twisting this way and that until my eyes flicked to a pool of blood that was spread out across the stone slab I'd been laid out on and tied to. I screamed in horror when I saw what should've been there, but wasn't.

I never gave a lot of thought to my hands, but suddenly, I was missing one. Atop the red puddle was my arm, gushing pure crimson at the wrist. I struggled against the ropes that held me down, but the air felt too heavy to fight against for prolonged periods. I writhed and spasmed on the slab, my bones aching with Vampiric hunger. My arm was in a dire state of distress, and my mind was taking the fastest train to Looney Town.

Cailleach crashed into the table, gasping in that way people did when they'd been stabbed through the heart in movies. Her cane whapped me across the ribs, but I think I'd reached some sort of pain maximum, because I could only feel the suffering in my hand, which wasn't even attached anymore. "Finish him, Kerdik!" she eked out, clutching her chest.

"Give me the ropes, Brìghde!" Kerdik struggled, letting out several noises of strain that sounded a little like heartbreak at having to fight his own father.

"Dian's secured!" Brìghde yelled.

"He's unconscious! Give me the other rope!"

The scuffle kept going, only this time Dother escaped Kerdik's hold and ran for the slab I was laid out on. He grabbed Cailleach's cane in two hands, lifted it and brought it down across my body, both of us howling like mad. He was Evil, and had Darkness and Violence as his brothers to show him the unlit path. My ribs felt either bruised or broken, but still my missing hand hurt the worst. At this point, I almost welcomed the distraction of Dother cracking me across the ribs for no good reason.

It wasn't the best way to meet my future father-in-law, but I was too deranged to hope for something better.

Before I could come down from the pain, Dother lifted the cane above me and started chanting in a language I didn't know. A sharp breeze picked up, whipping concrete blocks around the room, creating a dangerous cyclone to keep everyone else out. I was sprawled out on the table, unable to twist away as the end of the cane hovered above my belly. I felt like some sort of human sacrifice, unhinged from the pregame torture.

Dother slapped my lifeless hand onto my stomach, making me cry out not just from the pain, but with an indignant, *Hey man, I know that's not functional anymore, but it's mine!*

I didn't have time for anything but to brace myself. Kerdik was a green carbon copy of his father. Dother had Kerdik's same angular cheekbones, and eyes that made you think they could only be cold. But I knew better.

Kerdik's gaze could be warm – a trait I'm sure he must've picked up from his mother, since his father was a total wang.

Before Cailleach could steady herself and reclaim her cane, before Brìghde could intervene, and before Kerdik could make his way through the stone hurricane that was vortexing us right good, Dother brought the end of the cane down on my severed hand, and consequently, my stomach. I struggled against the ropes that held me captive for his whims, but having the wind knocked out of you by basically being pole-vaulted in the stomach rendered me completely useless.

So wrapped up in my own torment was I that at first I didn't see the crack that sizzled up a few inches on Cailleach's cane. Brìghde broke through the chaos, tackling Dother and knocking the cane from his hand. Her red curls flew out behind her, and her sunken-in cheeks were twisted with a look of "Let's do this."

Cailleach's cane clattered across me in the fray, but not before a crimson light shot out from the tip. I swear I saw a man's face in the glow – exaggerated black eyebrows painted across a red face with a hooked nose. The partial apparition rose from the end of the cane and moved to the ceiling. Then I saw him take full form, becoming a short, stout man instead of an amorphous, ghosty head. The crimson naked man laughed in triumph, and then darted out the broken window, laughing all the way.

Before I could warn anyone, fire exploded out from the

tip of Cailleach's cane, singeing my hip, and introducing me to yet more of the worst day of my life. I screamed and tried to stop, drop, and roll, but I couldn't so much as wiggle my hips. I saw nothing except the fire on my hip that I couldn't put out.

Then I realized it wasn't just my jeans that were on fire; the room was catching ablaze with errant cinders, and the vortex wasn't putting them out. The air fanned the flame, creating a whirlwind of molten orange and yellow with specks of blue that whipped around, heating the room in seconds. "Help! Kerdik!" I screamed, unsure if the panic or the pain was worse in that moment.

Dother laughed the signature cry of the evil villain. "Come, Carman! Your favorite son has set you free!"

Kerdik burst through the inferno like a friggin' fire-fighter on a mission. He made quick work of spraying my body with water, putting out the fire that had been content to munch away at the fabric of my jeans and heat the skin beneath. "Get Rosie out of here!" he shouted as he tackled his father.

Black smoke started to fill the room, making me cough as I spasmed from the blood loss and torment that never seemed to recede. I couldn't even bring myself to feel relieved when a man in a hoodie hurled himself in through the window. He beelined toward me to cut my bindings. "S'alright, Prim. I'll get ye out!"

I rallied at the sound of Lugh, though I couldn't see his face. He wore a gray scarf around his nose and mouth to keep from inhaling the smoke. One arm went under my shoulders, and another arm slid under my legs.

That was as far as he got before a blast of who knows what knocked the wall behind him, spraying the both of us with rocks that pelted the Good Samaritan on the back of the head. Lugh dropped me back on the table when he stumbled and fell, but this time I had the ability to move. Granted, I was delirious from hunger, blood loss, mutilation, unending agony, burns, and smoke inhalation. I didn't move all that far before I collapsed on the floor.

Of all the things to be able to see when I got to enjoy my few minutes of renewed sight, Cailleach's cane was right at my fingertips. Its owner was a few feet away, struggling to reach it with her weakened grip as she tried unsuccessfully to crawl forward.

"Please!" Cailleach begged me, and through my own torment, I could see the full breadth of her fear. Whatever was happening, she understood the ramifications of it better than I did. Though most everyone else saw her as the hunch-backed, wonky-eyed old hag, I could see her true form – a mid-thirties beauty with blue dreadlocks and determination burning in her eyes, struggling to right all that was wrong in the world.

Instead of reaching for my own severed hand that had fallen a foot away, I grabbed the cane and rolled it to her. Cailleach cried out in relief, and murmured a quick few words that made the cane stop glowing red. The fire emanating from the inside of the walking stick died immediately. The crack running down the wood wasn't crimson anymore, but a solid black lightning bolt of a scar that marked this dreadful day.

"Mother? Mother!" Dother cried out in anguish when the flood of fire ceased to add more fuel to the inferno we were still baking in. Dother was livid when it dawned on him that his mother hadn't been released from the cane. "Give me the cane! Carman, I'll set you free!"

"The rope, Kerdik!" Brìghde reminded him, lending her hand to the tumble of limbs.

We were close to victory, I hoped, but the moment Cailleach found the strength to stand, Dother decided he should cut and run. "This isn't over, you hag!" he growled at Cailleach, who, despite everything, stood like a woman of poise, looking like a frosty queen in the midst of utter wreckage. With that last threat, Dother vanished from Kerdik's grip and Brìghde's hold, leaving us to fumble through the inferno.

7

THE OLD FLAME THAT NEVER DIES

Everyone was pissed Dother had escaped, but I was still alternating between whimpering and out-and-out screaming. I couldn't find my hand, and that was no small problem. Despite the fact that I'd just been freed from the unforgiving slab, I crawled under the stone table, sobbing and writhing as I searched in vain for the broken parts of me. It was the worst time to get my sight back, and the most horrifying thing to see. My gaze kept flicking back to the empty space where my hand should've been, as if my eyes were on a tether. Blood was still oozing out, making me dizzy, but thanks to my stellar double-portion of life, didn't make me pass out. Consciousness felt like a cruelty in this situation, and I wished to close my eyes so I didn't have to see the horrific mess that my arm now was.

Lugh found his bearings and knelt down before me, his eyes wide with panic. "Kerdik! She's bleeding out!" he shouted into his gray scarf.

Kerdik stumbled toward us, shooting water at patches of fire at random, too turned around to properly focus on the blaze that surrounded us in a complete circle now.

"Lugh!" Brìghde shouted, the hurt in her voice almost palpable. "I thought you'd gone from Éireland!"

Lugh stood to address her, his chin raising like a man who could command even his regrets. "Aye, and I'll be gone again before ye know it, Brìghde. Just helping a friend." He knelt back down and hefted me into his arms, standing with agility and strength I just plain didn't have in the moment. I wanted to be strong. I wanted to be helpful, somehow lending a hand to quench the flames that raged at us from all sides. The only thing I could feel was torment. It was all I could do to keep myself from passing out. I prayed that somehow the bad guys were dead and gone, but knew better than to hope for luck like that.

"*She's* your friend? *She's* why you came back to Éireland?" Brìghde had just been fighting to save my life, but now, apparently, I was the other woman. Like we had time for crap like this.

"Kerdik's my friend, daft girl. I'm helping with Rosie because he asked me to, same as ye are doing. I'll not have ye painting a target on this one's back after ye just helped rescue her."

"Where are ye staying?" she asked as water shot from her palms at the fire. She was more on-point than Kerdik, who was still barely focused on his powers, and more on clearing his path to get to me.

"Put out the fire, Brìghde!" Lugh thundered. I was so woozy, I was surprised Lugh hadn't morphed into Andre Roussimoff in my imagination. Andre could rescue me any day. My rescuer was pissed, and didn't bother holding back. "Stop staring at me and deal with the fire! It's going to spread if ye don't put it out now."

"Don't yell at me!" Brìghde thundered, dangerous when scorned.

Lugh's voice softened to a seductive croon that made me want to blanche. "Don't ye want to keep me safe, Brig? Your love's in the middle of a fire, and he can't do nothing to save himself. Save me, Brìg." It wasn't panic, but a lover's plea. It was pure manipulation (but seeing as how I was also suffering from the business end of nearly being burned alive, I didn't protest dude's methods).

Brìghde renewed her focus on the flames, looking fierce in her elemental glory. The fire seemed sticky somehow, coming back to life even after it had been snuffed out in parts. It took three hose-downs for every section, requiring all of Brìghde's concentration.

Kerdik finally reached us, not bothering to hide his sickened look at my maimed arm. "Cailleach, Brìghde, do you have a handle on the fire?"

"Aye," Cailleach replied. "Get those two out of here." She narrowed her eyes at the man who still held me, like the pathetic damsel in distress I apparently now was. "I don't want to see ye around my sister for a good long time, understood? Brìghde is done with ye."

"Aye. I'm only here to help Kerdik. I'll leave as soon as this is all settled, and the Brothers of Destruction are locked up again."

"See tha ye don't make a mess of Éireland, like ye did the last time. Brìghde gave ye your eleventh toe. Best not be ungrateful for it."

It was such a weird thing to say, but Lugh didn't seem bothered by it. "Aye. Prim got peachy skin and a matching eye when she got her double-portion of life. I suppose I complained a wee bit too much about the eleventh toe that came from Brìghde's magic."

Cailleach tore her scowl from Lugh and softened her gaze when she met my unfocused eyes. "Ye helped me. I'll not forget tha."

Kerdik was in no mood to waste more time with pleasantries and drama. "I'm taking Rosie away so she can heal. If you catch wind of Dother showing his face in Éireland, summon me, and I'll be here to help. Thank you, ladies. Truly."

Cailleach nodded, since Brìghde was wholly focused on the fire. "Aye. Now, go. Keep the wee one safe. Dother won't stop until this is over, and it's far from tha."

Kerdik's hands were stained with my blood as he placed one on Lugh, and the other on the back of my head. "Close your eyes, darling. I'm here now."

It was the best thing I'd heard in a long time, so I took his advice, going limp as my body started to give up on me.

8

I TRUST YOU, KERDIK

When I opened my eyes again, we were in a cabin I wasn't familiar with. The wood filled my nose, but the soot was still in my lungs, so I coughed uncontrollably at the threat of fresh air. I felt like a total wuss.

"Lay her down, and run to the village to fetch Remy."

Lugh obeyed, gently surrendering my body on the floor of the cabin's living room. "Put pressure on her wrist, Kerdik, or she'll bleed out. It might take me a while to find him."

"Hurry!" Kerdik didn't look up as the door shut, but placed his hand over my mouth and vacuumed out the soot from my lungs, like a gentleman. "There. Now at least you can breathe." He flinched when he lifted my stump of an arm, and tied it off to stop the bleeding.

"K-k-kerdik?" I worked out, scared and very, very turned around.

He had real emotion twinging his usually composed features. I didn't like the look of fear on him, and wished I could lift my arm to rub the wrinkle that had taken up residence between his furrowed eyebrows. "Darling, I'm here. I'm right here. It's your Kerdik, and I won't leave you. Hold on, Rosie. Remy's on his way. He can help us."

He referred to "us" as being in pain, and I knew he meant that when I was hurting, it wrecked him just as much. That's what love did. I knew without a doubt that Kerdik loved me, and I very much adored him.

"Hurts," was all I could eke out. Sweat beaded on my forehead and neck.

Kerdik washed my face and hair without being asked. He squeezed my curls, rubbing the soot from them, and cooling me from the fire that I'd been sure I would die in. "I'll get you a pillow," he offered, making to stand.

"No!" I protested, my lower lip trembling. "I just want to s-s-see your face. Don't go."

Kerdik went from gentle to one tense, lithe muscle. He gripped my cheeks so he could stare into my eyes. "You can see me? You can see?"

I nodded once, which was all I had the strength to do. "Don't make me be w-w-without you."

"Never," Kerdik swore, his handsome features only marred by the soot stains that took away from the green glow I adored. "Always my queen. Here. I can at least help with one thing before Remy gets here." He reached into his shirt and pulled out a chain with a vial on the end. "It's from Bastien. We thought you might need it before I could get you back to him."

My eyes widened and my lower lip trembled. "Blood?"

Kerdik nodded. "Here. Let me help you." His arm slid beneath my shoulders, lifting me slowly when I screamed to warn him that slight movements were too much for my body. My ribs protested every hint of motion. Different levels of pain were starting to hit me now, making my body churn with an upset I couldn't muffle. "Easy, easy." He popped out the cork with his teeth and tipped the small bottle to my dried lips. Relief like I'd never known flooded through me, quelling a small part of the agony I was steeped in. It was barely two swallows' worth, but it was just enough to get my shoulders to loosen their stranglehold on my body. My tongue dipped into the lip of the vial, cleaning out every drop I could get. Kerdik brought the cork to my mouth, and I laved it clean, sucking on the brown, chewy sponginess to extract every last drop of sustenance. I whined when Kerdik took it away, wishing for a pool of the stuff. "You'll have much more, once you're healed."

"Healed?" I asked hopefully.

"I can't very well send you back to Bastien with one hand, can I?" He squeezed his fist a few times, producing a bunch of leaves that he then rolled into a little bundle about the size of a stick of gum. "Eat this. It'll take away your pain."

"Not if it'll knock me out. I n-n-need to see your face."

He looked on the verge of tears at my simple words. "I love you. This won't knock you out. It'll just numb you a little." He met my eyes as he fed me the herbs that smelled like sharp, black licorice and thyme. "I can fix this," he promised, glancing toward my hand. "Say, 'I trust you, Kerdik.'"

"I trust you, Kerdik." How very far we'd come that I could say something like that with utter confidence.

"I did this to you," he murmured with contrition in his eyes. The herbs worked quickly, and I could already feel the break in my ribs dull down to a petulant throbbing, instead of a debilitating injury. Kerdik kept me slumped against his arm, so I was half-sitting up, and could see the sincerity in his moody eyes. "I gave you this ring, and now you're... My gifts are always curses, but I promise, I didn't want this for you. I wanted to entrust the higher magic with someone who didn't have an inch of evil in her soul. I met you that first time, and knew I'd never seen a purer woman in all my life. I knew I could trust you, but I didn't pause to think that perhaps you shouldn't have trusted me. You shouldn't trust me to give you good things. Even my best intentions turn sour and wither eventually. I thought it would be different with you, that I could bless you without cursing you in the process. I love you, Rosie. Please believe that I didn't mean for this to happen!" He shook his head, disappointed with himself, and utterly awash in self-loathing. "I will fix this," he vowed again.

I wanted to hold his face, to comfort him, but I couldn't feel my fingers anymore. The numbing herb had the effect of too much alcohol, swinging me lower than I had the stamina to battle. "Don't leave me," I begged, scared of being injured and drunk like this in a place that wasn't my home. "He chopped off my hand!" I wailed, my jaw chattering in the throes of shock. "Your uncle chopped off my hand!"

"Yes, and now he's locked back inside the ring. I put a blessing on you so that if anyone, aside from me or you, tried to remove the ring from your hand, they'd be struck dead. Dian's immortal, so he was temporarily incapacitated. We took our window while he was down. Brighde and Cailleach distracted Dother, while I shoved Uncle Dian back into the ring. He'll not bother you ever again. Violence is gone from the land. Now there's only Evil to contend with."

"He chopped off my hand!" I repeated, still stuck in the loop of utter shock.

"You're white as a sheet, and you're shaking. Let me grab a blanket. I promise, I'll be right back. Not five seconds."

Before I could protest, Kerdik was gone, making tears well in my eyes. He held true to his word, darting back after about five seconds. "You left me!" I accused, blubbering and indignant. "I told you not to go, but you left me!"

Kerdik's mouth curved into a soft smile as he elevated my torso so he could hold me with minimal movement to my severely broken body. "And I came right back, as promised." He wrapped my body in a fluffy blanket, draping my wounded arm atop it, so as not to let the injury be brushed by the fabric. My eyes wanted to dart to the stump, but Kerdik turned my chin so my eyes focused on his. "You don't need to see it. It's temporary. I told you, I'll fix this."

"I believe you…" I meant to say his name, but my mouth went slack. My beating heart was the only thing I could hear, and the thuds were going too slowly, banging like a drum of doom before the last vestiges of soldiers gave up their noble fight. The last thing I saw was Kerdik's scared expression, the beauty of his face marred by the fear that something was irreversibly wrong.

I wanted to care that I was dying. I wanted to rally. I wanted my mom, and Bastien, too. I wanted so many things in that moment, but I couldn't grasp at any of them. I heard Kerdik shout my name, but I couldn't answer him. My life started to slip through my fingers, and I fell through the hopeless abyss of unconsciousness.

9

KERDIK'S WEAKNESS

It was my first dream in I'm not sure how long. I was used to spending my nights with Dub, but I guessed that he couldn't be near me anymore without his loyalties coming into question, now that Dian was trapped back inside the ring with him.

I dreamed about going on a joyride with Judah in some car neither of us were fancy enough to own. I took the turns too fast, laughing as we narrowly avoided a steep drop off the side of a cliff. Judah hooted and cheered, urging me to be more reckless, thrilling at the rush of danger. As far as dreams went, it wasn't too bad. I missed Judah, and hoped he knew nothing about any of this.

When I awoke, I wasn't on the floor in Kerdik's arms anymore. I was in a bed that wasn't my own. I felt the sheets, inhaling the smell of pine and a slight layer of dust.

That's the drawback of having slightly heightened senses –
you can smell thrill-worthy things like dust.

When my lashes fluttered open, I gasped that Dub still
hadn't taken away my ability to see. There was no pain
anymore, only a numbness that made all the bad things
seem like a hazy memory I'd just as soon forget. I studied
the ceiling, marveling at the honey-colored slats that were
perfectly aligned overhead.

I was still hungry, but my bones didn't ache as much,
and I could think without every third sentence being about
blood. I wanted to stare at my stumpy wrist, but only to
confirm that last night was a dream – some sick, twisted
nightmare I wouldn't have to deal with for the rest of my
life.

When I turned my chin, my eyes caught on a figure
sitting in a chair at my bedside. My gasp couldn't be
helped. I mean, dude had shoulders but no head. Well, no
head that was attached, anyway. Remy's head sat on his lap
like a cat reclining on its owner so he could watch me as
needed.

"Was it all real?" I asked, foregoing any sort of tradi-
tional greeting.

Remy leaned forward, his brown tunic pulling at the
waist. *"You can see me?"*

I tried not to grimace at the shiny, puckered pink skin
that had formed between his shoulders where his head
should've been. I nodded at Remy, unsure where I should
look when I spoke to him. "I missed you," I admitted. Even

though he was Remy the Monster, he was my knight, my healer, and my friend. He was *my* monster, and I loved him so very much.

"My Queen, you can't begin to understand how grateful I am that you're okay."

"Thanks, man. Kerdik, is he alright?"

As if waiting for me to mention his name, Kerdik strode into the room. His white dress shirt was clean but untucked, his sky-blue hair mussed in the back, and there was an untamed look in his eyes that made me worry he was working too hard. "I'm perfectly fine, love. How are you feeling?"

"I'm not sure," I admitted. "I don't feel much of anything. But I haven't moved yet, so that's probably why."

"He's lying, by the way. Master Kerdik's been completely distraught all night and all day. Even after he helped heal you, he's been irate with himself for allowing you too near the danger." Remy paused while Kerdik felt my forehead. *"He's really grown since I knew him in my first life. Never thought I'd see actual contrition from him."*

Kerdik's angular cheekbones and tightly pursed lips painted my vision with a glow of chartreuse, giving me something beautiful to gaze at while I let myself slowly wake up. With my good hand, I reached up and fumbled with the collar of his shirt, tugging him down so I could stare more closely at every single centimeter of his handsome features. "You're a miracle," I breathed, marveling at the feats nature had gone through to create a spectacular being like him. I couldn't help but be left breathless by someone so stunning looking at me as if I was... anything.

Kerdik closed his eyes as he pressed his forehead to mine. "Leave us," he barked at Remy.

"I guess some things about Master Kerdik's temperament might never change," Remy chuckled to me.

After Remy exited, shutting us in the bare room alone, Kerdik sank to his knees by my bedside. He sandwiched my good hand between his, kissing my knuckles as if in prayer. "Of all the retched things I've done in my life, I regret you meeting my family the most. They've done nothing but cause you harm. It's because you love me that they did this to you. You're my weakness, and they won't stop targeting you to make me dance for them." He squinched his eyes shut, as if in physical pain. "And I wouldn't hesitate to dance for you. I think..." He swallowed hard, working his way up to some confession that was stuck in his throat. "I think I'm a danger to you, being who I am, targeted by the Brothers of Destruction as I've been."

"Kerdik, that's not your fault. All you did was love me. You didn't ask them to kidnap me. You didn't ask Dub to blind me."

"Be that as it may, all those things still happened. It's because you're tied to me. Rosie, I have to let you go. Until all this is over, I can't see you anymore."

My eyebrows shot up into my forehead, and then lowered, furrowing with distaste. "What? That's not the solution."

"Your hand was cut off last night because of the ring *I* gave you! My blessings always turn to curses. It kills me that my love keeps raining down chaos on your head!"

"Kerdik, stop this. We had a bad night. You're all turned around because of seeing your father, and the battle and all that. You'll feel differently in a few days. Don't make rash decisions like this."

Kerdik kissed my wedding ring. "You're married to Bastien. Even if all those other things weren't true, I'm afraid I'm not the man we both want me to be. I die a little inside every time he kisses you. Every time I see the need in your eyes that longs for him, I see myself killing the man you love – perhaps both of them. You're my queen, but you're still his princess, and it kills me."

This point, I couldn't protest. I didn't want to hurt Kerdik or Bastien, but I knew that's exactly what I was doing by keeping them both. As symbiotic as things often were, I think we all knew there was a shelf life to the homeostasis. "I've been unfair. This whole arrangement's cruel to both of you."

Kerdik shook his head. "No. You didn't ask for a double-portion of life. I knew you loved him, but I wanted to keep you anyway. Our arrangement still stands. I'll come for you after Bastien's life is over, but I need to step back for a while. I gave him enhancements so he could keep you safe. But he has no chance of doing that if I'm around, bringing danger ever nearer."

Tears welled in my eyes, clouding my vision as I

grasped at straws. "I live at the castle with all the people you need help from. You need Urien, Lot and the Untouchables. You can't not see me. You need me! I calm you down! You can't go off to fight your father alone."

Kerdik softened and moved to sit on the edge of the bed. He washed my tears away and dried my face. "I can't do this anymore. I feel like my heart's going to leap out of my chest every time you trip and fall. I have to think of Avalon now. She needs me, and I can't have my focus so divided."

"But I'm helping you with Avalon! You can't cut me out now. This is every bit as much my fight as it is yours."

I tried to sit up, but Kerdik gently pushed my shoulders back into the mattress. "You can't get up, darling. You need to lie down. The herbs I gave you numbed a good portion of your body. If you stand now, you'll fall, and I'm afraid my heart can't take it."

"Kerdik, don't do this. Don't leave the second I can finally see you. I need you!" I cringed at the admission, but it was true. I was down a hand, and had a lot more to do, as far as getting Avalon back on her feet. "You need me, too!"

"I do, but needing is a luxury. I don't have the spare energy for extravagances like that anymore. I have to get my father back inside the ring. I have to deal with all that's escaped from Cailleach's cane."

I inhaled sharply. "Carman didn't get out, did she?"

"No. Not even close. But something almost as sinister leaked out, along with a few other creatures. I have to find them and shove them back into the cane. I can't stop or rest until that's done, and you, my dear, are quite the distraction."

"Wait," I pleaded, panicked as he pulled away. "Wait! You don't mean right now, do you? You're not leaving this very second. I have buckets of arguments you haven't even heard!"

Kerdik chuckled, standing to gaze down at me with affection that made him look like an angel in the flesh. "I want you to call me if there's danger that comes for you, understood?"

"I can't!" I wailed, utterly beside myself. "They cut off my hand, so I don't have your ring anymore."

Kerdik tilted his head at me, a wry smile on his face breaking through the pained expression I hated seeing on him. He reached over my body and carefully slid my injured arm from under the covers.

Only it wasn't injured anymore. I let my gasp fly free as I took in the details of the hand I'd missed. I wriggled my fingers, shocked that such a thing was possible in this rural setting. "How? But I saw... And then he... How?"

"A little of Remy, a little of my blood. There's nothing I can do about the scar, though, I'm afraid."

My gaze fell on the black stitched line on my wrist. It made me look like some sort of Frankenstein experiment. I shook my head to stop the vain assessment. I had both hands again; that was all that mattered in this equation. I wriggled my fingers and made a fist, relieved my hand still served its basic functionality. "You fixed it."

"Just as I promised I would. Honestly, it was touch and go for a while there. I wasn't sure Remy would get back before your severed hand started dying. But all's well now. He said you should have full use of it, too."

"That's... I can't believe it. I mean, this is beyond a Band-Aid, for sure. You gave me my hand back?" I gaze up at him, enraptured by his beauty. That he wasted the magic of his smile on me blew me away every time he bathed me in his sweetness.

Kerdik backed away from the bed, wary of me, as if I was dangerous. "You can't look at me like that, Rosie. I mean it. I want to see the glow of adoration in your eyes too much. You're trying to make me stay, when I've just said I can't."

I wanted to argue so very much, but all that would mean was that I wouldn't be respecting Kerdik's wishes. I'd be telling him who I wanted him to be, instead of who he was clearly telling me he needed to be. Kerdik had grand adventures ahead of him, many of which had nothing to do with me. In lieu of an argument, I opted for kindness. "Who are you taking with you?"

"Cailleach and Brìghde are in the next room with Lugh and Remy. I'll take Cailleach and Brìghde with me. It'll go faster if we work together to find all the evil and destroy it. Lugh and Remy will stay with you until Bastien gets here. Then they can do as they please."

"I want you to be more careful."

Kerdik scoffed at me. "You're one to talk."

I ignored his sass. "You keep throwing yourself into these dangerous situations, thinking it'll all be cool because you're immortal. Well, you're fighting another immortal now, so brace yourself and have a plan."

"Are you actually lecturing me?"

"Yes, and you'll hear every word. You can't think like a single man anymore. If we're going to be married someday, it matters if you come to me in one piece."

"Now, now. You're the one who was in two pieces yesterday." His lips drew to the side as he tried to erase his cheeky grin. "That was probably inappropriate."

I squinted one eye at him. "Yes, well, thanks for putting my puzzle pieces back together. I'm starting to hit my limit with how much can go wrong at once."

"Is that all, then? Cailleach and Brìghde would like to get going. I promised them we could leave as soon as you were awake."

"No, that's not all. Stay away from Dother, Kerdik. I mean it. Dude's one evil guy, and I don't want you near him. I don't even understand how you guys shoved Dian back into the ring, but I doubt we'll catch the same lucky break a second time."

"Ah, now that I can explain. Dian tried to take away your ring when he removed your hand. Do you recall what happens when someone tries to steal your ring?"

"Morgan's soldier died when he tried. But Dother can't

die, can he? Remy was explaining it to me, but I'd only just woken up."

"Dian was knocked unconscious, so I was able to stuff him back into the ring. We were quite fortunate he acted so impetuously, assuming I'd only planned for the usual means of robbery."

"Yes, how very lucky your asshat uncle chopped my hand off."

"We're one down now, which is more than we've been able to say in almost two years. Despite it all, we're in a very good position. There's the slight hiccup of the Nain Rouge escaping from Carman's cane, but that's nothing for you to trouble yourself with. Brìghde is going to handle him."

"Speaking of things escaping, did Seirbigh get dealt with after he found you?

"I slaughtered him as soon as I finished with your letter. There's no place for Kelpies in Faîte." He let out a heavy sigh. "Come, let's get you dressed. The others are in the living room. I can carry you there. If you saw something, we need every detail."

"Okay." I couldn't even sit up on my own. My arms worked to some degree, but from the waist down, I was completely limp. I clumsily flung the sheets off of me, revealing my bare legs and one of Kerdik's shirts I'd been dressed in. I tried to move my legs to swing them over the edge of the mattress, but I couldn't even rally the smallest muscle from my ribs to my toes.

Kerdik didn't say a word as he grabbed a pair of jeans from atop the chest in the corner. Slowly, with enough seduction that it felt as if he was undressing me rather than putting clothes on my body, Kerdik slowly inched the jeans up my legs. He kissed my unfeeling skin inch by excruciating inch as he slid the pants on me. I couldn't feel him sucking on the inside of my knee, but the sight was a beauty to behold.

After he buttoned my jeans for me, his eyes hovered above mine, bringing his lips tantalizingly near as he braced himself on all four limbs, hovering over my body. "I was so scared," he admitted, whispering to keep his confession between us. "When I saw you strapped to that table, I..." He shut his eyes. "It was the one time blindness would have been a mercy. I don't ever want to see you and my father in the same room again. The sight was... I simply cannot bear it. You are everything left in me that's still good, and he's every evil thing in the world."

I angled my chin up, silently asking for the kiss we both needed. We'd been through too much, and were about to separate for too long. His lips were like velvet as they moved slowly with mine. I wanted to beg him to devour me, but I think we both knew that after the beating my body had been through, tenderness was best.

No one knew how tender Kerdik could be, but I got to see his veil of arrogance folded back so that there was nothing between us. I got to see the raw preciousness that a man in love radiates when he's kissing the woman he can't let go. How I wished Kerdik would never let me go. How I wished for an eternity of his soft, delicious kisses to suck on and savor when the world around me was ugly and mean.

"I want you to stay away from Dother," I said between kisses. "And you should take a multivitamin. It'll keep you healthier. I told you to before. Are you?"

Kerdik snorted into my kiss and then pulled back, balancing on his elbows atop me. His grin was handsome when it was sincere. "I love how you love me. I don't need a vitamin, darling; I'm immortal."

My lips drew to the side. "Still. You should take one, just in case."

He kissed me again, gently, and with the promise of a return someday. "As you wish it."

10

PLANNING FAÎTE

"Tha's not a plan!" Brìghde argued, throwing her overlarge hands into the air. "Seeking out destruction in a land tha's fraught with it isn't going to get us anywhere."

Cailleach was unbending. "We can't give Dother time to regroup. We should split up, for certain. I can seek out the Nain Rouge and suck the wee bastard back into my cane. Brìghde, ye can see to rounding up the Werewolves in Éireland. Kerdik, ye can go after Dother."

I wanted to speak, but there were too many people bickering over what needed to be done, and in which order. I'd been laid on the couch, my feet on Remy's lap. His posture was rigid from trepidation at there being too many immortals in one place. Kerdik was known to be volatile on occasion, but Cailleach was known to curse people on a dime, and Brìghde, I was coming to learn, whined a whole lot. Remy had already lost his tongue and his head, so he didn't make a sound, though I could hear his disgruntled opinions flickering through his mind.

I learned we were holed up in Lugh's home, which I'd stayed in for several days before. Seeing it was a whole different experience. It was a log cabin with no frills, save for a fireplace, and a roughly-hewn mantle that had etchings of fiddles carved into the thick edge. He'd been out getting firewood, so I hadn't been able to put a face to the man yet.

Remy's head was perched in his over-the-shoulder sling, hanging in front today so he could look out at the others from where his head hung at his navel, resting atop my feet. I tried not to stare, but dude, it was freaky. It was still him, though, which was the important part.

When the walls of the cabin began to shake, I gripped the arm of the couch and did my best to stand. My measly effort was muted by the fact that my legs were still mostly asleep. "Okay, enough. Calm it down, guys. Whichever one of you is making Lugh's house shake, knock it off." I squinted at Kerdik, knowing he was the culprit.

"You shouldn't be standing yet," Kerdik admonished me, clearing the distance between us to lower me back to the couch, halting my pathetic attempt.

There were a million questions I could've (and probably should've) asked, but I couldn't think past the one that started it all on its head. "How, Kerdik? How did they kidnap me? I thought no one could port into the castle."

Kerdik swallowed hard. "They didn't port. They're pure evil and violence. They mostly used violence to barge in the old-fashioned way and strolled right through the front door. A fair bit of soldiers were lost, but most survived, a little the worse for wear."

Of course the soldiers took a hit. When war happens, it's always the many who suffer for the wicked ambitions of the few.

"The mayapple root, did it... Are the Vampires cured?" I asked as I scrunched my toes, unable to take it if we'd gone through all this for nothing.

Kerdik pressed a kiss to my forehead, blessing me with tenderness to counter the cruelty we'd all endured. "Yes. It all came together beautifully."

Cailleach, Brìghde and Kerdik started up their argument again, but thankfully kept it slightly less acerbic, now that I was part of the conversation. When the three started to simmer instead of boiling over at each other, I pitched in my two cents. "I don't want you going after Dother by yourself. That's not safe."

Kerdik shot me a look that told me he thought I was being cute. "Darling, I'll be fine. You worry too much."

"Dother's the biggest bad guy out there right now, correct? Then outnumbering's the key. I can handle the Werewolves, so take Brìghde with you."

He glowered at me. "I can't imagine what argument you might whip up that would make that something I would consider. I'll not feed you to the wolves."

"What's Brìghde going to do with them? No offense, but this ring's the only thing that can suck the dangers of the mutation out. Brìghde has better things to do than play sheriff right now. Bastien and I can figure this one out. The Untouchables can corral the Werewolves, if they're still up for helping out. You need backup against Dother."

Brìghde put her hands on her hips. "Finally, a decent idea. Seriously, Kerdik, I'm not going to run cleanup in Éireland while ye go off and smite Dother. I want to help deliver the final blow to him for all he's done."

Kerdik's jaw tensed. "I don't care which job sounds more glamorous to you. I care that the job gets done. End of story."

Brìghde rolled her eyes. "I love how ye say 'end of story' and expect tha to actually hold up. We're a tribunal, Kerdik."

"See what you did?" Kerdik said to me, looking more frustrated than anything else. "You and Lugh got lucky with those two Weres. That was a controlled setting with plenty of escapes."

"Then we'll set more traps," I concluded with a shrug. "I can help, Kerdik. That's why I'm in Faîte. If you don't need my help, then I'll go back to Common, where I belong."

Kerdik nodded while Cailleach balked. "Yes, I think that's for the best. You should go back to Common, where it's safer."

Cailleach balked at him. "Nowhere is safe! Then Faîte

has half the chance it needs, Kerdik," Cailleach argued. "Think things through. Rosie's shown she can handle herself. If her end of things gets out of control, she can call you or me." She inclined her head to me, offering her rescue services, should I need them.

I inclined my head to Cailleach. "Thank you."

Remy stood, lowered my feet to the cushion, and slapped his fist to his chest. *"Where Rosie goes, I go. I'm in touch with several of the Phare Dullahan. I'm sure they can be persuaded to offer their assistance, as well."*

I relayed Remy's promise, but this didn't seem to instill any sense of relief in Kerdik. Cailleach was onboard, though. "Aye, we'll accept tha help. Thanks, Healer."

Arms akimbo, Brìghde sighed in Kerdik's direction. "Very well. Is tha better now? Shall we get your doll a house of pillows in case she falls? Ye baby her, Kerdik."

I half-expected steam to come billowing out of Kerdik's ears. His fists were clenched at his sides, and he stammered out several half-protests before he bellowed out, "No! I forbid it. Most of those people were there with her when she was abducted in the first place, and they couldn't do a thing to stop it! You'll go back to Common, Rosie. I'll entertain no more discussion about it."

Part of me wanted to laugh in his face at the notion that anyone could put their foot down and send me to bed without supper, but the other part of me knew Kerdik was afraid. He loved me, and sometimes that love didn't know how to come out looking like a bouquet of daisies. I tugged on his sleeve, bringing him down to kneel in front of me so I could look him in the eye, and pretend our conversation was private. "Hey, I'll be alright. Lugh and I work pretty well together, and you know that where Bastien goes, Link or Mad are sure to follow. Plus, there's Nolan and Malone. I've got Remy and who knows how many others, too. What are you worried about?"

"You! Have I not made that clear? My concern is that you live long enough so that we have our chance at a life together. I don't want you maimed before you get to me. I don't want you to see your friends mauled, either."

My mouth drew to the side as I studied his worry. "I love you, mister. If you didn't care about me, you'd see that this was the right move."

His voice softened with a caress of pain. "But I adore you. This isn't happening."

My grin finally won out as I smoothed the worry wrinkle from between his eyebrows. "Oh, babe. It's so cute that you think you can tell me what to do. I love that after being alive for so long, you still have a little naivety to you. It's endearing."

Cailleach chortled at Kerdik being overruled without me having to raise my voice at all. That's the thing about refusing to fight; you win every time.

11

LOU VAN GUARDEN

*T*hree light kicks to the bottom of the door announced that someone was here. When Remy opened the door (since my legs were still being wusses, and the immortals couldn't be bothered with things like answering doors), a man strolled in, carrying several armloads of firewood. He had short dark hair that was messy on top, letting its natural slight wave do all the hairstyling for him. He had a toothpaste ad smile with perfect, gleaming teeth, and just enough self-assured sleaze behind his grin to really do some damage on any nearby females. He looked to be in his late twenties and set the piles of firewood on the hearth with no sign of struggle under the burden of the load. "So, where are we at with everything?"

There was something familiar about him, but I couldn't place it. I'd seen him grinning before, polished and together. Maybe with an airbrushed background? The image my brain kept skipping to was a photo of this same dude with a glossy finish and a sexy smirk to him. But where would I have seen a photo of him in Faîte? They didn't have cameras here. Yet as I stared, I knew I'd seen his wide gait and the rolled-back shoulders, only for some reason I was picturing him in a leather jacket.

Cailleach explained my division of the chores, as if that was the plan we'd all agreed upon. Kerdik scowled at her, but didn't object this time, knowing this was the best way. "So if you're still in, ye will stay with Rosie, and help her cure the Werewolves."

"Grand." The stranger rubbed his palms together in anticipation of the showdown. "Are ye ready, Prim?"

A giant "duh" dawned on me when I put the voice to the face, gaping at him. "Lugh? This is you?"

"Ye got your sight back? Tha's grand, Prim! Oh, I'm so glad for ye."

"That's what you've looked like this entire time?"

His face cracked into a wide grin. "Aye. Disappointed, are we?"

A second "duh" smacked me over the head. My mouth fell open, and I didn't think I could be more bowled over if I tried. "You're Lou Van Guarden! You're Lou Van Guarden from Lost and Forgotten! You're not Justin Bieber," I accused in shock.

Lugh tilted his head back and belted out a loud laugh as I pointed at him. "Aye, tha's me."

"I have all your songs. The entire catalog," I admitted like a true fangirl. "Your 'Jessica' album? My all-time favorite." I didn't think about my baby deer legs; I tried to scramble to standing, but gravity played its dirty trick.

Kerdik caught me before I conked my chin on the floor and lowered me back to the couch. "Easy, darling. Your legs won't work for at least another hour or so. Careful, now."

"You're friends with Lou Van Guarden?"

Kerdik quirked his eyebrow at me. "Yes. So are you. You two fought Werewolves together." He pried at my eyelids to check my pupils. "Did you hit your head during the battle or something? Are you alright?"

"How are you not freaking out? He's only like, the most famous bass player in Common. But he can do so much more than that." My eyes cut to Lugh, and my clumsy finger pointed at him with purpose. "You hold the songs together, but they're totally wasting your talents, keeping you solely on the bass guitar. Judah and I were at your show in Cali a few years ago. You did this interlude where you played the trumpet, then the piano, then an upright bass, then the violin, then the trombone, then the drums, then the harmonica. I had no idea anyone aside from Blues Traveler could rock a harmonica like that. You blew my mind, dude. Then they just put you back on the bass, which don't get me wrong, you rocked, but total waste. Then the lead singer, Finnegan McCabe, plays like, three guitar chords any dummy could bang out, and everyone cheers." I threw my hands in the air to demonstrate my frustrated state with the situation. "Nonsense."

Lugh snickered at my animated monologue. "Wow. I think I like this version of ye much better than the one who calls me Justin Bieber. I don't mind playing bass. Success in the music industry is about how everyone fits together, not how grand I am. Tha's how the band works best, so I play where I'm needed."

I grimaced. "Oh! I called you Justin Bieber. I think I made a joke about you having a small penis!" I buried my face in my hands. "I would never have done that if I knew who you were."

Lugh abruptly stopped smiling. "Don't ye dare stop being who ye are just because of who I am. Most fun I've had in ages was palling around the pub with ye. Where's the sharp-tongued lass who put me in my place and told me to stop being so full of myself?"

I groaned at myself. "Me and my big mouth."

Steam started billowing out of Brìghde's palms, which felt like an ominous warning for everyone to shut up. "You've seen him naked?" she spat at me.

"What? No! I only just got my sight back at the battle."

Remy placed his hand on my toes. *"Careful, Rosie. Lugh's a Gancanagh who worked his magic on Brìghde. It's been decades, but she still burns for him."*

Lugh rolled his eyes. "Are ye daft, Brìghde? Rosie's married, plus she belongs to Kerdik. I'm not so reckless tha I'd steal Kerdik's future wife. She was only taking a jab at me." His eyes cut to Kerdik's to make sure his bestie believed him.

Kerdik wasn't the least bit perturbed. "Brìghde, you're being irrational. Lugh isn't stupid enough to try anything with Rosie."

I held up my hands. "I promise, Brìghde. Nothing happened. It was a dumb joke, is all."

Brìghde lowered her hands, and the steam only came in short spurts now. "Grand. Keep your hands off Lugh, wee queen. I've no problem sharing Kerdik, but I'll not tolerate ye getting your hooks into Lugh."

"My hooks?" My head swiveled with attitude.

"I think it's time we split up," Cailleach suggested. "This is the most time the two of ye have spent talking since your marriage ended, and I fear it's been a few words too many. Lugh, stay with Rosie and wait here with her healer for Bastien to show. Brìghde, Rosie will be with her husband, so no one's going to seduce Lugh while you're not here."

I gaped at Cailleach, who shot me a "these dumb kids" kind of look that told me to just go with it. I closed my mouth to shut my indignation inside.

Kerdik sighed as his gaze cut toward Brìghde. "Alright, let's get out of here before you make a complete fool of yourself." He leaned down and brushed his lips to mine, giving me something beautiful to hold onto. "I'll be back for you to say a proper goodbye once this is all taken care of. I'll always come back," he promised in front of the entire room.

I looped my arms around his neck and used the leverage to pull myself up to sitting. Well, it was mostly slumping, but it was the best I could do. Kerdik's arms banded around my back and secured me to his body to keep me upright as he sat on the edge of the couch. "Be safe," I urged him, worry overtaking me and trumping my embarrassment at being all lovey in front of the viewers. "Don't go anywhere without Brìghde. I mean it. And I was serious about taking a multivitamin."

Kerdik's chest vibrated with mirth. "Of course you were." His gaze turned serious as he studied my face. "I love you, darling."

"I love you." I kissed him once more, savoring the slow pleasure that rippled through me. "I don't know how I got so lucky."

"Lugh, I love ye! I never stopped in all these years apart!" Brìghde blurted out in desperation.

Lugh inhaled the burdened breath of weariness and let it out with practiced patience. "Aye. Let's go have a chat in the other room."

12

DUB'S CURSE AND CAILLEACH'S GIFT

fter the two left for the bedroom, Cailleach cleared her throat. "Kerdik, I need a word with your wife." She was very specific not to use the term "future wife" with me, but considered our marriage already a done deal. Kerdik gently lowered me to lay on the cushions again, and stepped back so Cailleach could speak to me.

"What's up?" I asked with as pleasant an expression as I could manage through my mild discomfort at being so thoroughly useless.

"What ye did in the battle? I saw ye lost your hand in the rubble, but ye returned my cane to me instead of searching out your own missing part. Ye did me a great service, not using the cane for your own gain. I understand what drove Kerdik to put tha ring on your finger now. Ye have a pure heart. Not many would forsake their own right hand to return a cane to an old hag. Dother wanted to use it for his own plans. Many others have tried to steal my cane from me to get more power. But ye didn't want to steal my magic. Ye didn't try to summon Carman, either, like Dub wanted ye to."

I didn't mention that I wouldn't have the first idea how to do something like that. "Of course not. It belongs to you. When I was blind, I would've been pissed if somebody stole my cane."

"Ye went against a Brother of Destruction. Dub gave ye an order, and ye disobeyed."

I frowned, wondering if that would be problematic down the road. "I guess so, but he knows I'm not down with the possibility of letting Carman out."

"Ye say it like doing the right thing is a simple task. It's not, and I see valiance when it's right in front of me. Thanks, Rosie."

"No problem, Callie. I'm glad it all worked out."

Like a crack of lightning in my heart, I felt some foul thing smack across my insides. In the next breath, the room went dark. I screamed, my arms flailing as I started freaking out. My body slid off the couch until I was writhing on the floor, howling my anger at Dub for pulling such a rotten trick. "Stop it! Stop controlling me! Give it back!"

Kerdik and Remy moved to my sides to cage me in, Remy prying my eyes open to investigate. *"No! It happened so quickly. Rosie, I can't combat blindness from a Son of*

Carman. I'm sorry!" I heard his monologue of self-loathing prattle on, but I was too lost in my woe to comfort him.

"He can hear me," I told the room in a voice that couldn't be anything but mournful. It was the false hope that the worst of it might be behind me that stabbed my heart in unmerciful ways. "No, Dub! I can't unleash Carman! I can't risk that. You know I can't! Stop doing this to me!" I lost my sense of direction and self, rolled over and started banging my forehead on the hardwood floor over and over, punishing him as much as I could for imprisoning parts of me that I very much needed. I couldn't think of another way to hurt him, other than harming myself.

Kerdik jerked me around and rolled me onto my back, but I shouted all the more, fighting him, the air, Dub, and the unfairness of it all. "Rosie, it's okay!"

"No, it's not okay! I can't see you!" I thrashed in Kerdik's arms, throwing a tantrum I didn't have the grace to be ashamed of. This was the straw that would break my spirits, I could feel it. This was the injustice I couldn't suffer graciously through anymore. "I can't keep going like this! I can't keep being jerked around by whoever wants something from me. Dian wants something, so he kidnaps me and takes my hand. Faîte wants the Vampires gone, so I have to leave Common and live with my dad, who hates me! Dub wants the cane, so I get to live my life blind until I obey him." Anger the likes of which I couldn't damper down rose up in me like a punch to rival the great Andre Roussimoff himself. "I'm not a pawn to be used up and thrown out! I'm a person, and I want a normal life! I want bowling night and grad school. I want to see my mom and watch bad TV!" My arm broke free from Kerdik, so I raised my fist in the air like the madwoman he'd reduced me to. "Screw you, Dub! I hope that cane burns, along with everything you want for Faîte. I hope you burn!"

Remy was frantically trying to help Kerdik secure me, so I didn't bang my head all over again. I don't know why they cared. This was my choice. I had precious few things that were up to me anymore, but I should've been able to bang my head as much as I felt like it. I wanted to hurt Dub somehow, and this seemed like the best option.

Kerdik resorted to squashing me to the floor, his body pressing down atop mine, my back to the hard wood. Lugh and Brìghde wandered out to see what the commotion was about, but I didn't care to explain anything to them, or calm it down for the viewers. Kerdik was at a loss, scrambling to contain my angry fists that beat at the air, as if that might free me from everything I raged against. "Rosie, you have to stop! You can't knock yourself out like that. We'll find a way around Dub. We'll find a way around cracking open the cane."

"I don't care anymore! I won't be controlled like this. It'll never end! Even if you manage to kill Dother without the cane's help, Dub will find another reason to jerk me around. If I'm unconscious, the darkness is *my* choice! *He's* not closing my eyes, I am! I need that choice, Kerdik. Give me that choice!"

"The choice to give yourself a head injury? Darling, I need you to calm down. You'll see this isn't the way."

"I can't do this anymore!" The scent of lavender and something else wafted to my nose, filling the room with a sweetness that hadn't been there before my freak-out. "Are you trying to drug me? Are you making me calm down? That's not my choice! Stop making choices for me! Stop controlling me!"

Kerdik was at a loss, frantic at making the wrong move when he was just trying to help. "You can do anything you like, except for hurt yourself. You're a week without your *lueur*, so you're not thinking clearly. You think you're standing up to Dub, but he doesn't care about that. He knows he's winning, and that's all that matters to him."

Cailleach's voice broke through my whirlwind of chaos. "Kerdik, let her be. She's being expected to keep up with immortals on two different planes of existence, without being able to see what's coming at her. When everything's aimed in her direction, it's bound to take its toll."

I breathed through my nose like a bull when Kerdik moved off of me.

I heard Cailleach's skirts rustle about her legs as she knelt at my side. Her hand on my forehead was soft, like velvet. Something about her presence soothed my palpable ache. I leaned into her touch, missing my mother in the worst way. Lane would know what to do. She would take one look at the situation, make an executive decision, and that would be the end of the drama. She wouldn't let me be sacrificed like this.

Cailleach was gentle with me when I was two steps away from devolving into a lunatic. "Wee Rose, how easy it is to forget that you're paying for all our sins." Then to Kerdik, she asked, "Ye said she's a week without her *lueur*?"

"Yes. Her husband, Bastien the Bold, is on his way here. That should help a little. But the blindness, Callie. I can't do anything about the blindness."

I heard a manly clap of a hand on Kerdik's shoulder, and then Lugh's voice reached my ears. "We'll figure it out, Kerdik. It's all of us against one measly immortal. Give it some time."

Kerdik was quiet, but his regrets carried through the room. "It's been nearly a year he's been toying with her sight. Dub isn't the type to construct a plan with holes in it. There will be no getting around this. Either I do as he says and risk Faîte, or my bride never sees my face again. She's the one person who looks at me like... like... No one's ever looked at me the way she does."

"Aye, brother. Let's not give up hope yet. You've been selling her on the 'it's temporary' logic. Best not abandon tha now. At least, not in front of her."

Cailleach leaned down and spoke low in my ear. "I can't grant ye your sight back, but I can help with your fight to cure my people from their curses." She grabbed onto my hands, lacing her fingers through mine and marrying our palms together. Then her silky grip turned to a vice without warning, her breath cold on my nose. "Take a little of me with ye. When you're afraid ye might be attacked when you're out hunting Werewolves, hold your palms out at them and will the cold to blast out from ye. It'll be enough to chill their bones, so their movements won't be as quick. Then ye can get away before ye get mauled."

Brighde gasped. "You've never shared your power with anyone before. Why now?"

"Because she's commissioned herself to clean up our land. She's done so without being asked, and without the proper tools. If I'm to hunt down the Nain Rouge, then I want to be able to leave the Werewolf problem behind, so I can focus on my task." Cailleach gripped my hands tighter. "Plus, she could have her sight right now, if she'd taken my cane for herself and done as Dub commanded. Instead, she sacrificed her sight to protect Faîte. A little ice is the least I can do."

I was about to protest, but my fingers turned frosty in the next second, and it seemed my lungs filled with ice as I inhaled. My exhale brought about a freezing gust that I could feel chilling my lips and teeth. When she released my hands, my breath was normal again, though I was no less confused.

I willed myself to put my panic behind me as best I could. I'd thrown my tantrum, and now it was time to cowboy up – blind or not. Dub could screw with my sight, sure, but he couldn't change who I was deep down in my core. That limited panic attack was all the power I would grant him to have over my emotional state. If Lane was here, she would remind me to know who I was. I wasn't the girl who writhed on the floor like a maniac. I was a woman. More than that, I was a queen, and I had a job to do. The neighboring country was in a state of chaos and needed my help. I could rise to the occasion. What's more, I could sit up, probably. Maybe.

Remy saw my pathetic effort to sit up and met me halfway. He worked his hands under my shoulders and propped my back up to rest against his chest. I could only guess his head was swung in its sling around his back or something. *"Easy, now. We'll figure this out. Cailleach's gift is going to be a big help."*

I covered my face with my hands, breathing in and out for a few beats before I ventured opening my mouth. "Thanks for the ultra-freeze rays, or whatever it's called. I'm sorry I... I just don't know how to fight back against Dub anymore. Knocking myself out seemed the best way to go."

Cailleach moved to kneel before me, and for an errant moment, I wondered if she had old lady knees beneath her skirts, and if kneeling hurt her. She positioned my hands to aim at the couch. "Move aside, Kerdik. We'll have ourselves a little training session before we're off." She explained it all to me again, speaking calmly, like a patient teacher. I did my best to rally and focus on the tasks I could handle, rather than the problems that threatened to crush me.

"Just pick a focal spot, point and shoot?"

"Tha's the idea. Try and freeze the couch for me." She patted the cushion behind her and then stood, walking away from the blast zone. "Okay, give it a go, then."

I brushed my hair from my face and held my hands out, aiming my palms in the direction of the couch. I closed my eyes so that the darkness was my choice, and not Dub's. Cracking my fingers a few times, I centered myself, shutting out Kerdik's nervous breathing, Brìghde's whispers to Lugh that this was a wasted effort, and Remy's stream of consciousness. I needed to find myself in the chaos. I couldn't see myself, but I needed to locate the spark that made me come alive and stay that way. My chest ached for so many things, but one element no one had managed to strip away was the ins and outs that made me... me. My heart found its steady rhythm, beating out a rap I could sense in my bones – even if I still couldn't feel my legs. My head swayed back and forth with the beat only I heard, and with a slow inhale, I pushed my will out from my palms.

I wasn't sure what I expected to happen. Maybe nothing for my first try. Maybe, at most, a little puff of fog, like when you exhaled on a frosty day. I didn't expect my palms to burn with a freeze that felt like a knitting needle through the center of my palms, nor the outbursts of surprise that cracked out around the room. "Did I do it?"

"What were ye trying to do?" Brìghde shrieked. "How much power did ye give her, Cailleach? Tha's way too much!"

Cailleach's voice dinged with surprise, but she maintained her womanly deportment all the same. "She's shown she can handle more magic than the average Commoner. I've no doubt she can learn to manage this. Though for a first try, I'll admit, tha was surprising. I wasn't expecting ye to be able to shoot tha soon."

I frowned. "Did I do it wrong? Did something happen?"

Kerdik slowly draped my arms around his neck, so he could scoot me forward. He took my hand and placed it on what I thought was the couch but felt hard and cold. "You turned the couch to ice, darling. It's a solid block now. I'd say that's about five inches thick here."

I grimaced. "Oh, whoops. That was too much, then. How do I undo it?"

"The same, but in reverse. Suck the cold back into your palms. But I can do it for you, dear. Tha part's tricky."

I shook my head. "No. I can try. I made the mess. I should clean it up."

"Could we practice on something else next time?" Lugh complained. "I'll be running out of places to sit."

"I could always practice on you," I suggested, with a mischievous wiggle of my eyebrows.

Lugh chuckled. "No, thanks. Jays, I wasn't expecting ye to do tha."

I closed my eyes again, trying to find that part of me that remained unadulterated and unadulted, which seemed to be the trick to staying me. Too much of my life revolved around being a grownup. I needed play. I needed soccer, bowling, and dorky dance contests with Judah. I needed the me I'd been before all of this.

I bit down on my lower lip and willed the cold to come back inside of me. The same jarring needles pierced through my palms again, and this time there was a cold that traveled up my arms to my elbows.

"Okay, stop! The fabric's smoking now. You've melted the ice well enough. That was good, Rosie."

"Brilliant, tha was," Lugh remarked with clear admiration in his tone. "Can ye grill a sandwich like tha? Because tha's something I could use around here."

My eyebrows pushed together as I considered Lugh's off-the-cuff suggestion. "Can I start a fire like that?"

Cailleach placed her hand on mine. "Ye can, if ye focus hard enough. But tha takes a fair amount of magic. Best not be draining yourself too much when you're still on the mend. When you're able to walk again, practice on the firewood. After a bit of patience and luck, ye might be able to start a small blaze. First the freeze, then the melting, then the fire. Ye don't have the magic to start a fire at random without going through the proper steps first."

I felt my fingers, marveling that they could do something so cool. "Thanks, Callie. Once I get the intensity part down, that'll be crazy helpful. You're right; I'll be able to slow down an attacker if the Werewolves get too near. Not to be a constant whiner, but healing the cursed is harder than it looks when I can't see what I'm doing."

"Well, now ye have help. My gift in ye won't last forever, mind ye. It'll fade in time, but it should last long enough to help ye through this rough patch. And remember to summon us if ye get stuck, and your *Guardien* can't get ye out of trouble. We need ye to succeed, so we can come home to a land tha isn't in shambles."

Kerdik leaned forward and kissed my knuckles. "I have to leave now. We've given Dother a good enough head start. It's time he was brought down and put away for good."

"Okay. You'll have Brìghde with you?"

"Of course. You don't need to worry about me." Then he spoke over his shoulder. "Not out of your sight, Lugh."

"I promise. She'll be safe here." Lugh's arm slid around my shoulders, and his other arm coiled under my knees. "How about we start with getting the Queen of Avalon off the floor? I've got these new-fangled things called chairs in the kitchen. They're all the rage in Éireland."

"'Chairs', you say? What are these contraptions of which you speak, kind sir?" I replied, putting on my best sophisticated foreigner voice.

Brìghde's shrill voice cut through our attempt at levity. "Put her down, Lugh! She can walk well enough on her own without ye having to put your hands all over her."

Cailleach spoke for me, which was good, because I

wasn't super well-practiced in dealing with jealous women. That's the blessing of growing up with a hump and a wonky eye. You're not a threat to anyone's relationship (or non-relationship, as it were). "Brìghde, Lugh's not your concern anymore. He can put his hands on whomever he chooses. And Rosie can't walk, actually, so he's only doing as Kerdik asked, and looking after her."

"I can give walking a try if this is making Brìghde uncomfortable."

"No," Kerdik, Remy and Lugh ruled. Then Kerdik said, "We'll be going now. Bolt the doors until Bastien comes. You've got enough arrows in your quiver, just in case?"

"Aye. I've got arrows enough for every monster who makes a grab at Avalon's queen."

I rolled my eyes at the liberal use of my ridiculous title. I couldn't see, couldn't walk, and couldn't even get to my own country to rule it, as I was supposed to be doing. I didn't feel like much of a queen; most days I felt like a joke at best, or a dying workhorse at worst.

"Ye aren't going to send me off with a proper farewell?" Brìghde asked sulkily.

"See ye around, Brìghde." Lugh's fingers dug into my body in what I could only guess was a protective hold, as if trying to keep me from Brìghde's wrath. It was hard to keep up.

Kerdik took charge of the room. "Remy, go on and gather the rest of the Dullahan who'll help us. Leave the ones who are going to be problems. We don't have room for any more of those. Phare Dullahan only."

Lugh carried me to the kitchen and sat me down on the chair, securing my head to his hip so I didn't topple over.

Remy made his way in behind us and scooped up my hand. *"I'll be back by morning, Rosie. Tell Bastien I hope to have at least a dozen cooperative Phare Dullahan with me when I return."*

"Will do. You're sure you're okay with this, Remy? You kind of got drafted without being asked."

I could hear the smile in his reply, which warmed me to my healer even more. *"I didn't need to be asked. My queen needed her knight, so I'm here. It's as it should be."*

"I don't deserve someone as good as you fighting for me. This is your second life, Remy. You should be sipping margaritas on a beach somewhere, not using your new shot to dodge arrows and fight off monsters."

"I'm exactly where I want to be, and you'll not worry another moment about it. I'll use my second life how I choose, and this is what I wish."

With that heroic declaration that no one heard but me, Remy exited, leaving a pang in my heart. If someone so pure of intention was fighting for our team, then just maybe we had a shot.

13

NATIONAL DONUT DAY

"I can't imagine why you left her," I sniggered as Lugh slid a chair closer to me at the kitchen table and lowered himself onto it. My body was still unstable, so he looped his arm around my shoulders and secured me to his side. Now that I'd had a chance to glimpse my surroundings, I felt a little more confident being upright in the cabin. I could guess well enough where things were, and since I was anchored to my seat and to Lugh somewhat comfortably, I didn't wobble as much as I did when I couldn't picture where I was in space.

"Jays, I forgot what a pill Brìghde can be. I used my Gancanagh abilities on purpose once, Prim. Once. I thought it would be a power move to seduce an immortal. I got a double-portion of life out of it, but much of it's been banished to Common, so it wasn't all tha well thought out. You want my advice on marrying an immortal?"

"Marriage advice from you? Hmm. Let me think about that."

"Have an easy out clause, like what Kerdik did for me, seducing Brìghde so I had an excuse to leave. Every time I remember tha I was almost stuck with her for a century and a half, I'm grateful for tha green bastard."

"Kerdik's not like Brìghde, and I didn't seduce Kerdik with magical witchy-woo. We fell for each other the old-fashioned way."

Lugh gingerly lifted my right hand and fingered my aquamarine. "Right. A bloke gives a strange woman from a foreign land a ring the size of an iceberg the first day he meets her, and it's love at first sight. I think there's a movie about tha one."

"Oh, shut it. We're not like you and Brìghde. End of story."

"Maybe end of *my* story, but yours hasn't barely begun."

"Speaking of stories, hold the electric guitar, Batman, you're Lou Van Guarden." I threw my arms out to the sides, as if daring him to explain himself.

Lugh chuckled that he'd been outed. "Aye. Guilty as charged. It's the perks of being Gancanagh. Things come easier to our kind. I don't have to practice an instrument more than a few days before I've mastered it. I'm the best shot in the land, after the rest of my kind were snuffed out. I can learn most trades or skills with minimal effort, so I can fit in just about anywhere."

"That's pretty cool. Man, what I wouldn't give for things to come easy to me." Though, I immediately felt guilty for complaining. Maybe school didn't come easy to me, but soccer did.

"The downside is tha I get bored quickly. Tha's why I've been able to stick with music for so long. The girls are always new, the songs are always evolving, and there are so many instruments to choose from. And even though I've mastered how to play them, there's still the new challenge of making them all fit together into something palatable."

"Sounds like you've found your niche. No joke, but your concert in Cali? Totally blew my mind. Might want to talk to your lead singer about not doing the princess wave anymore, though. I'm a legit princess, and I don't even do that."

"Aye. Finnegan says it's his thing."

"Can't argue with solid market research like that."

"Ye aren't half bad to spend the day with, Prim. How's the hand?" He cradled my right hand in his palm, running his thumb over the black stitches.

"I'm kind of dying to test out a good old cartwheel to see if it's up to snuff, but I've never done one blind. Plus, I'm sort of maxed out on injuries at the moment."

"Kerdik gave ye his blood, ye know." I heard him sip his drink.

"Uh-huh. It's how I got to have the double-long life in the first place. Same as Brìghde did for you."

"Kerdik's never done tha for anyone but ye, and now he's done it twice."

I nodded but didn't say anything else. I sensed he was working up to a point, but I wasn't sure I wanted to hear it. I offered up a bland expression to let him know I wasn't about to take the bait.

"He let ye marry someone else. Tha's the part I don't understand. Tha's not the Kerdik I know. He likes to take what's his and ignore the rest. Your husband's upright now, is he?"

"You'll meet him soon enough. Kerdik even blessed Bastien. Gave him enhancements to help keep me safe."

"I've been away for a long time. Never thought I'd see the day Kerdik loved anyone enough for tha."

I cleared my throat. "I think there's a whole universe of crap we can talk about that isn't my love life. Are you seeing anyone?"

"I'm seeing everyone, and tha's the way I prefer it."

"Are you happy?" It wasn't an accusation, assuming that kind of life would grow unsatisfying. I had no real idea what it was like to be the only Gancanagh left, and to be granted a double-long life on top of it all.

"Ye know? I am. Jays, no one asks me tha. In my regular life in Common, I'm content. There's enough new adventure to keep me pushing myself, and enough perks to where I don't get overwhelmed or feel deprived. Faîte, on the other hand, just isn't for me anymore. Too much magic makes a world turn sour. Plus, I like technology. I like central air. It's the little things tha feel like big things, and I don't take them for granted."

"Makes sense. For what it's worth, I'm glad you're happy. You're good at it. I had fun with you at the bar, before the whole Werewolf nonsense broke loose."

"You're a good wingman. I had fun, too." We sat in comfortable silence for a few beats.

I tested my toes by wriggling them to see if I could feel the movements but felt only the smallest stirring.

My head jerked in Lugh's direction when out of the blue, he said, "Your Da's a fool to cut ye out like tha."

"Hello, where'd that come from?"

"You're a good person. Most people either drool over the rock star life, or they criticize it. No one bothers to ask if I'm happy."

I smirked at him. "Could I get a drink of water? I'm not sure my legs are totally functional yet, or I'd get it myself."

"Sure." He stood and moved to the cupboards. I heard the glass clunk on the counter, and the water being poured from a pitcher. "How about ye? Are ye happy, Prim?" he asked as he set the glass down in front of me. I felt around, but had a hard time locating the cup. I felt like a dummy, wrapping my fingers around nothing over and over again. "Here. Sorry about tha." Lugh molded my hand around the cup. "I'm not grand at helping out a blind person, I guess."

"Well, I'm not great at being blind, so no judgment here."

"Are ye happy, Prim?"

I took a drink, quirking my eyebrow at the question. "I can't remember the last time that mattered. Happiness is for people with options, and right now, that's not me. Faîte's up a creek, so here I am. I don't think it's any little girl's dream to go blind, leave her home, get kicked out of her dad's life, spend most of her time in a dungeon puking her guts out, get her hand cut off by her future father-in-law, and then go off to help animalistic Fae who probably want to tear her face off." I set my cup down carefully, not remembering how tall the table was, and not wanting to crack the glass. "But I'm sitting here, having a drink with Lou Van Guarden, so there are bright spots enough to get me through." I stuck my finger into my water, and within three seconds of concentration, the whole thing was turned to ice. "Oh, man. That's sweet."

Lugh considered my words, and then slapped his hands together. "Let's go sledding."

A real grin broke out on my face, but then fell. "Dude, I can't see well enough to walk. I'm sitting up well enough on my own now, and I can feel my toes finally, but I don't think I can even walk yet. I can't imagine sledding's on the approved activities list."

"Cailleach and Brìghde are in Éireland now, so the seasons will go back to normal eventually. Best enjoy the snow while we have it. Can ye stand yet?"

I picked up my foot and stomped it with some

certainty. "I think I might be able to, but no Olympic racing yet."

He reached across the table and placed his hand on mine, making me startle a little at the contact. It was difficult to interpret touch when I never knew when it was coming, and I couldn't see the person doing it. Lugh's words were sincere and made me hang up a few of my excuses for the promise of adventure. "I can't let tha sad recollection be what ye remember of your first life. Life is about moments, and right now, we're going to snatch up a grand one. I've got a sled in the shed tha'll fit two. I can steer us and keep us away from smashing into trees and whatnot."

"Is it safe to go outside?"

"It's not even twilight yet. The Weres don't come out until nearly midnight. The moon has to be overhead."

A grin I couldn't stifle broke out over my face. "Really? We can go sledding for real?"

"Sit tight. I'll be right back with winter gear. Ye can't go out without a jacket."

I sniggered at the scolding, noting that he sounded like a dad, rather than the sexy, rogue recluse the press made him out to be.

He returned a few seconds later, kneeling down to slide my feet into boots that were from the pile of things Kerdik had sent him to pick up for me. He even went so far as to lace them up, and then brought my hand down to run my fingers over the fur that lined the top and the inside. "Feel how soft tha is? Kerdik was very specific ye have the best."

"Wow, that feels like a cloud. He's a sweetie. I'll have to bring him some bubblegum next time I go to Common. It'll blow his mind."

Lugh snickered, and then helped me to stand, letting me balance using his arm. I could kind of walk, but it wasn't super organic or graceful. Lugh didn't make fun of me, but wrapped my coat around my shoulders, holding it open while I threaded my arms through. He even went so far as to button it for me.

"You don't have to do that." I don't know why it made me shy to have him tending to me so sweetly.

"You're terrible at being a queen. You're supposed to have maids and attendants to dress ye and do all sorts of things for ye. This is the minimum; ye should demand more."

"Are you my handmaiden?" I teased. "How'd I get so lucky?"

"Aye. Until someone else comes along, I'm your handmaiden."

I laughed at the cuteness and took a chance to reach out and place my hands on his biceps, feeling his jacket, and then migrating to his shoulders. I wanted a clearer picture of the man who was being kind to me after such a rough battle. My fingers flitted over his face, picking out the features I could visualize from the articles I'd read about Lost and Forgotten, and the album covers I had on my playlist to get me through life's lulls in Common. He had thicker eyebrows, and short hair that had the tousled look only a stylist could achieve without making a guy appear messy. I felt his strong jawline, coasting my fingers over his cheekbones to feel his light smattering of stubble. "Prettiest handmaiden I've ever seen," I teased, wondering how I'd stumbled into a cabin with Lou Van Guarden. "I guess life can't be all bad, if we're going sledding and all."

"Tha's the spirit." He took my hands and brought my palms to his lips, so he could press a kiss there for me to hold onto. "Can ye feel tha?"

I nodded with a shy smile. "I've got full use of my hand, thanks to Kerdik."

"Aye, he's a thoughtful lad." He pressed my palm to his cheek, so I could feel his face again. "We're the only two of our kind, ya know – half-immortals as we are. When all this is over, we should keep tabs on each other."

I tilted my head at him. "Do you think you could see my smoke signals from across the ocean? We don't exactly live on the same continent, Lugh."

"Ye forget about cell phones."

"Ah, right. So if it's two in the morning, and I want someone to talk to about the intricacies of life, you're on my call list?"

"Only if it's two in the morning, and only if ye can work pancakes into the conversation. I'm a sucker for a good pancake." He moved my palm over his cheek so I could feel the scratchiness. "If it's two in the morning, and I get a grand idea for new song lyrics, I can call ye up, and you'll pretend it's the greatest thing ye ever heard?"

"That's the thing about friends who hold onto each other." I closed my eyes, a pang of worry gnawing at my insides. "We'll make it through Faîte, right?"

"Aye. We'll have our two in the morning, Prim." I could hear the grin of a bright idea in his reply. "Ye should come on tour with me for a while. Bring your husband."

I smiled, my eyes lighting up. "Well, twist my arm. Do you have anyone to spend the holidays with?" I couldn't imagine a single dude with no living family in Common would have much to come home to.

"Not a single soul. I usually spend it in a soup kitchen, ladling out hot soup for the homeless. It looks good for the band, sure, but really, I do it so I'm not alone at Christmas."

"How about you come stay with Bastien and me for Thanksgiving, Christmas, and National Donut Day."

Lugh laughed. "National Donut Day? I don't think I've been celebrating tha one properly."

"That can be remedied. Judah, Lane and I make a huge spread. I mean, so many donuts, you can't eat another one for a full year, until the next National Donut Day. Then the party revives. We make them all from scratch. Like, caramel apple-filled ones, pistachio eclairs, and there are contests, too."

"Contests? My, I have been missing out."

"You're telling me. There's a best taste category, and a

weirdest donut one, too. Bastien nearly barfed when he tried Judah's bologna and ketchup donut. It was the one time everyone wished they were a vegetarian, like me." I grinned at the memory. "National Donut Day, holidays, and pretty much any day you want some downtime. I'll keep a room made up for you in my house."

I wasn't expecting Lugh to hug me over something so small, but his arms crushed me to him with a tenderness that told me he'd been lonely for far too long. He didn't want a woman to settle down with, but instead he needed a family who was there when he needed to recharge. "Cheers, Prim."

"Hey," I said quietly, hoping to soothe a little of the ache in his chest that was now palpable after being exposed to the air. "Hey, it's okay. You're not alone. I'm here for you."

He kissed my cheek before releasing me, and I could hear the rapture and elation in his tone. "National Donut Day it is, then. I'll clear my schedule for it when all this is over."

"But first, sledding."

He molded my hand around his forearm, and we started out on our little break from the serious things that threatened to break us down. We weren't a queen and a rock star here. In the late afternoon in Éireland, we were just us, and somehow, that was more than enough.

14

SLEDDING WITH MY HANDMAIDEN

If you've never gone sledding while being blind, I'm not sure I'd recommend it. As much as I wanted to trust that Lugh wouldn't let us crash into a tree, I was still getting to know the dude. I closed my mouth through a scream as we flew down the hill that probably wasn't all that steep in real life. I couldn't tell how high up the top was, but the slope felt harrowing with no frame of reference to go by. My nails dug into Lugh's wrists, assuring me that both my hands were working at full capacity now.

When we slid to a stop after a long period of coasting, Lugh was laughing at my fright, his chest shaking my back. "I told ye I wouldn't let ye crash. Ye don't have to hold on tha tight. It's like you're afraid I'll launch ye into space."

"When I get my sight back, I'm blindfolding you and shoving you down a hill on a plank of wood to see how totally in control you are."

"I still wouldn't scream like a wee lass."

"I'd be willing to put money down that you would."

We'd been sledding for a while now, but I knew Lugh wanted to go another round. "Let's see if it's better if you're facing backwards when ye go down."

"How's that going to work?"

"I face front, but ye face me. Maybe ye won't scream so much if ye can't feel the wind on your cheeks."

"Okay, one more time. But then we go inside. We've got to get ready for Operation: Wolf-out."

"Aye. One more, then." He picked up the sled with one hand, and wrapped his other arm around me, tucking me into his side so I didn't fall. I held onto the buttons of his coat, walking in-step with my head tucked under his chin. "Do ye make hot cocoa at Christmas with your family?"

I grinned, my cheeks lifting slowly from the cold. "With melted candy canes in it. We have a gingerbread house contest that lasts the week before Christmas, too. Judah gets super competitive with his. He's got such a technical mind. Actually gets out graph paper and makes an interior for the thing. It's intense."

"I've never made a gingerbread house before."

"Well, you won't be able to say the same thing next Christmas. Lane usually gets frustrated with hers and ends up using gingerbread-flavored graham crackers, the cheater."

"What was yours last Christmas? A little cottage for two?"

I swallowed the lump in my throat. "It was stupid. It was supposed to be our castle in Province 10, where my dad lived. I even built him a throne so he could hold court with all the little gingerbread men."

"I'm sure he would've loved to see tha."

I shrugged, and clung tighter to Lugh as the wind picked up around us. "If he wanted to see it, he would've been there. He has a real castle with real subjects; he doesn't need gingerbread." *Or me. My dad doesn't need me.*

"Well, *I* need gingerbread." The sweet wistfulness in his tone warmed my cold heart. Lugh squeezed me as we made our way up the hill. He laid the sled down and sat atop it, taking a moment to situate himself. He patted the spot between his legs, so I could hear where I was supposed to sit. "Facing me, this time," he reminded me, reaching up his hand to guide my awkward bumbling.

It was a bit more intimate, being face to face. Even though I couldn't see him, I could feel his gaze. Slowly, Lugh positioned my legs to wrap around his waist, and brought my cheek to press against his stubble. My body tightened when his lips brushed against the shell of my ear. "Your Da's a fool. He's made the wrong decision and doesn't know how to undo it now."

"It doesn't matter. I had a dad for a while, and it was everything I imagined it would be. Not everything's meant to last forever, I guess. I just didn't think we'd have such a short shelf life."

"Aye. Hold onto me, Prim. And keep your head on my

shoulder, otherwise I won't be able to see where we're headed."

I obeyed, indulging in the snuggle I needed. I wasn't good at talking about my dad. I had enough sadness and loss in my life without adding him to the mix. I'd lost friends to death. They were the ones I would save my tears for, because if given the choice, they would still be here. Even after his death, Remy sought me out.

That was love. That was family.

Lugh scooted us toward the point of no return, snaking his hand under my coat so he could give my side a little squeeze, just to freak me out more. Boys are charming like that. It wasn't until we were almost over the edge that I heard the voice that made everything in me rally. "Rosie? Who is that? Get your hands off my wife!"

"Bastien!" I cried out, but it was too late. Lugh and I slid down the hill, picking up speed at a faster rate than the other times we'd gone down. The wind whipped at the back of my head, racing by me far quicker than I'd been anticipating. I clung to Lugh, my teeth chattering as I tried to muffle my shriek at the thrill of adventure.

Perhaps this would be my great adventure – finding the fun moments through the harrowing ones. What a life's purpose that would be, chasing after the good, just to have something to giggle about.

We seemed to go on forever like that, gliding even farther after we plateaued in our winter wonderland.

"Hold onto me!" Lugh warned. "I'm tipping us so we don't crash!"

"What?" was all I worked out before Lugh's hands abandoned the sled and wrapped around me. He did a hard lean to the left, dumping us out of the sled, and smooshing us in the thick snow. My shriek slowly died down into fits of giggles as I rolled away from him and faced upwards. "That was the best one! Okay, the next time we go sledding, that's the way to do it. I don't know if we were more aerodynamic that way, or if it was just a different sensation going down backwards. Either way, that's my vote."

"I'll make a note of it," Lugh said, his voice cracking. It sounded like he was lying next to me, also facing the sky. "We almost crashed, but I tipped us in time. I didn't think we'd coast tha far. Are ye alright?"

"I'm better than alright. I went sledding." I couldn't stop grinning at the things I didn't know I could still do, limited as I was. "This time last night, I was holding my severed hand while I bled all over a stone altar. This is way better. Maybe if I'd known sledding was in the cards for me in a mere twenty-four hours, I wouldn't have belly-ached as much over a tiny flesh wound."

Lugh snorted. "I'd like to see ye pass tha off to your husband as a tiny flesh wound. I wonder what you'd consider a serious injury."

"Bastien doesn't need to know about it." I lowered my

voice in the universally understood "be cool" tone. "He'd freak out, and he doesn't need the stress. He's got enough on his plate."

My body stirred at the sound of my husband calling for me. It had been too long since I'd heard his voice. "Rosie! Are you okay?"

I lifted a thumbs-up into the air. "All good, babe. You miss me?"

"Only every day. Whose neck do I need to snap for letting you go down the hill like that? Nearly gave me a heart attack."

"This is my new handmaiden, Cross Shot."

Lugh chuckled as he sat up. "Grand to meet ye, Bastien. Wait up there; we'll come to ye."

The walk up the hill had been arduous all the other times, but now that Bastien was back, it was barely a stroll. I was sweating from the exertion, but I didn't hold back as I crashed into Bastien's arms. He was shaking with need, even through his winter gear. My stomach screamed at me to bite him, but the vial of blood Kerdik had given me kept my brain from fogging over and going into rip-tear-kill mode. "I missed you."

"You look hungry. Let's get you inside." I knew by his hurried and staccato movements, that he really meant, "I'm horny beyond reason. Let's get you out of those clothes."

I smiled at our need and hoped it would always be on

the same level as food for us. Lugh led the way to the cabin, where I was barely able to tell him we needed a few minutes before Bastien tugged me into the nearest bedroom.

15

MADIGAN'S APOLOGY

There was nothing like the touch of Bastien, except maybe the taste. Both satiated and excited me in equal measure. Both made me want to never stop indulging in them. Both made me crave more – always more. We made love three times before there was a knock on the door. "Yeah?" Bastien exhaled, his hand stroking the curve of my backside.

"It's time to go. It's going to be midnight soon, so wrap it up." My satiated spirits perked up at the sound of Madigan's voice. I'd thought Bastien had come alone, but knowing we had another Untouchable on our team played heavily in our favor. "And if you're going to be carrying on so loudly, at least bring cotton for us to stuff in our ears. I don't need to be hearing ye climax from two rooms over, Bastien."

"I'm not that loud," Bastien grumbled, sitting up. He

sponged off using the water pitcher and basin, and then helped me do the same, which started a quick but passionate round four.

Madigan was not amused.

Lugh applauded us when we finally emerged, to which I gave a cheeky bow. "I feel like I should give ye a hug, mate. Tha's some impressive stamina. I don't think I've ever gone three rounds in half a night before."

My guilty blush must've been evident. I held up four fingers to Lugh and stretched my palm out for a high-five.

"No! Four? Four times? Well done, mate. Well done!" He slapped my hand and then clapped Bastien on the shoulder, I guessed.

"Yeah, yeah. We're ready now. Kerdik mentioned we'd be finding Werewolves and curing them with Rosie's ring. What resources do you have here?"

"I've got my share of weaponry. Take anything ye like, but the bow and quiver are spoken for."

I frowned. "We don't want to hurt them. I was thinking more nets and luring them into humane traps or something."

"The weapons are for self-defense. We may not want to hurt them, but they'll be wanting to take a chunk out of us, tha's for sure."

Mad tapped something on the floor, and then huffed in frustration. "Ye don't have to be stubborn about it. I know it's my fault ye passed out from too much healing back in the dungeon."

My head jerked in his direction. "Huh? What am I being stubborn about? No one's pissed at you, Mad. I healed Annabelle because I wanted to. Where is she, by the way? Is she alright?"

"Aye. She's grand. She's with Link and Quinn back in Avalon now. They're rounding up the Werewolves there to get them ready for ye." He huffed at me. "Ye aren't upset with me?"

"No. Why would I be?"

"Then take it!"

"Take what?"

"I fixed this for ye."

"Huh?"

Bastien intervened, interrupting our awkward exchange. "Mad, she can't see. You have to tell her what you're doing." Bastien was patient with his socially-stunted friend, but firm in how I was to be treated.

"Oh, right. I brought ye this. Made a few enhancements to make up for... ye know."

I frowned. "What is it?"

Bastien sighed, taking my hand and placing it on the handle of my cane, which apparently was the source of Mad's consternation. "Oh, my cane! That's so great. Thanks, Mad. I've been needing this. Oh, man. Watch me go with this thing. I won't have to cling to anyone anymore."

I could hear the dismay in Bastien's voice. "This better not backfire. I like when you hold onto me."

"Sure, but now it'll be my choice, not what I have to do." I kept my arm wrapped through Bastien's, and held my cane with my other hand, grateful for the choice that was finally mine. "Thanks, Mad." I tapped it to the ground a few times, noting it felt heavier than it had when I'd first used it. "It feels different somehow."

"Aye, tha's what I was telling ye. I fiddled with it, so now ye aren't so helpless."

I pointed my chin in Bastien's direction. "Care to decode?"

Bastien moved his fingers over my thumb, anchoring it to a button a few inches from the handle that hadn't been there before. "Feel this? It's a little trigger that when you push it, blades pop out around the lower foot of your cane. You can use it to fight off attackers, if you need to."

Lugh made a noise of appreciation, but I was thunderstruck. "Seriously? You weaponized my cane? That's... That's badass, Mad. Thank you. Show me?"

Bastien pressed my thumb down on the button, and I heard the "shink" sliding sound of metal. "Careful now. Mad doesn't believe in using dull blades. These are pretty sharp." He lifted the cane and slowly brought my fingers to touch the knives that jutted an inch out, and then angled downward two inches. There were a dozen that I counted, arranged in two rows of six.

"Mad, this is crazy. Are the edges serrated?"

"Aye. I didn't want ye to have to do more than one swing. Best catch them right the first time."

It was Madigan's version of a bouquet of flowers, and I appreciated them as such. "Thank you. You didn't have to do that."

"Ye didn't have to heal my Annabelle." He let out an exhale that sounded like it had been trapped inside him far too long. "Ye told me ye needed to rest, but I didn't listen. I couldn't see straight. They told me to put her down when she got infected. When I heard ye could help, I didn't stop until I brought her to ye. I didn't think."

"You love your daughter." I don't know why the declaration felt like a slice to my innards. "You're allowed to be a bad friend for a minute if it means you're a better dad to her for a lifetime. I get it."

Bastien was not thrilled with my blasé reaction. "Yes, well, that's not happening again. It doesn't seem like the Werewolf healings were too strenuous on her, but the capture's going to be rough. Malone and Nolan can help with that, though."

"Oh, they're here?" I grinned that we had a decent-sized team that was assembling.

"They're out doing a patrol of the grounds, making sure you're safe. Now that we're inside, they're setting up traps to make sure nothing gets at you while you're staying here."

"Wow. That's nice of them. But it's cold outside. You sure they don't want to come in and warm up?"

"Nah. They don't tire. I mean, part of that's because they don't need sleep, but the other part's pure dogged determination." Bastien slapped his thigh. "Dogged? Get it? Man. Never gets old."

I mimed a laugh at the cheesy pun. More than the slight upward swing of the conversation, I was grateful my guy still had enough of himself inside to be able to muster up the wherewithal to make a joke. "What've you guys been up to over there?"

"I'll grab the gear, and then we can go," Mad said, not needing the update.

"Rounded up a few more Vampires that eluded us the first time. Maybe only a dozen or so. Lot's got his hands full with the Sombre Dullahan, so I don't want this to take too long over here. Let's pound out this Werewolf problem in a few days, and then get back."

I furrowed my eyebrows. "I don't know how feasible that is. It seems like we should help out with Dother or the Nain Rouge when we finish up here. Lot's got soldiers to help him out still, right? Nothing's happened to the army?"

"The what?!" Bastien exclaimed, taking a few steps back. "The Nain Rouge is in Faîte? Since when? How have I not heard about this?"

"Well, it like, just happened last night. I can't imagine word travels that fast around here."

"You're telling me the Nain Rouge is roaming about Éireland?"

Lugh backed me up. "Aye. We were in a big fight with Dian and Dother. They stole Rosie, so the immortals showed up. Cailleach's cane opened for a second, and the

Nain Rouge came out." Bastien balked and started hurling questions. I could hear Mad's boots stomping toward us in his usual irate manner, but Lugh continued as if there had been no interruption. "Dother and Dian stole Rosie from ye in her castle after Kerdik knocked her out with the mayapple root."

"We knew she was taken from the castle, but we didn't know who took her, or where! What did they want with you, Daisy?" He spoke the nickname, but it didn't have its usual sweetness to it. Bastien was in overprotective mode, so I let his panic play out how it best suited him.

Lugh didn't bother with answering Bastien's many questions; he simply continued on with his account of things. Bastien did a fair amount of yelling, accusing, and cussing out Kerdik, who wasn't there to take his verbal beating. The only time I spoke up was when Lugh mentioned the bit about Dother cutting off my hand. "Dude, I thought we agreed Bastien didn't need to worry about that."

Bastien let out a cry of anguish and indignation that I would try to keep something so big from him. He lifted both my hands, as if he expected one might be missing, and he hadn't noticed this whole time. He traced the scar around my wrist, a noise of distress pinging both our hearts. "This wasn't supposed to be your life," he finally said, utterly heartbroken. "I was supposed to be able to give you a good, long life. Nowhere in the plan was your hand getting chopped off, or you being anywhere near the

Nain Rouge. We took vows, Rosie. I promised I'd take care of you. This isn't a well-cared-for woman. You had magical surgery, and I wasn't even there for you!"

"Hey, whoa. None of this is your fault. It's alright honey. After this nonsense is over, it's you and me. We'll go back to indoor soccer and the bowling league." Though at this, I frowned internally at the false hope that Dub would ever let me go.

Bastien got me, feeling my internal swings. His arm banded around my shoulders. "I can't wait for exactly that. Let's go, then. Let's free the Werewolves from their curse and get out of here."

"Baby, you've never been sexier than when you talk like that."

TREACLE TRACKS

I'd never been hunting before, but something told me I'd be terrible at it. The weaponry the guys wore made me nervous, since I knew it might be used on people who couldn't access their higher reasoning skills. It was counterintuitive to make as much noise as we could while we tromped through the foot-deep snow toward the footbridge.

Mad was frustrated at the lack of action thus far. "Are ye sure this is the best place to find Werewolves? Seems like we should be hitting up anywhere tha's got a lot of people gathered."

Lugh was firm. "Aye, but not many gather anymore at night, since the Weres have been attacking. Best cut them off at the source."

I nodded, backing Lugh up. "I remember Declan

swearing that this was where he'd seen too many people passing through – themselves on one side, but by the time they crossed over, they had the Were gene. If we figure out how they're being made, that'll at least stop more from coming at us. Otherwise we're trying to fill up a leaking bucket. No point."

I could hear Bastien's frown. "I guess. I hate to think that more and more and more Werewolves are being made. I was kind of wishing there'd be a cap on the madness at some point."

I shot Bastien a smile I hoped he could see in the lantern's light that Mad carried. "See? That's what I love about you. Always believing in fairytales. It's sweet."

"Who's Declan?" Bastien asked.

"Some dude we met at a bar, right before I ran into these two love muffins."

Bastien grumbled as I leaned down to pet Malone and Nolan. Since the moon was up, they were in their wolf forms. I'd protested at first when Malone had brought me a rope, asking me to use it as a leash so he could guide me. "It's so demeaning," I'd protested, worried that I was putting a grown man on a leash. It seemed icky somehow, like something Morgan might do.

In the end, Malone and Bastien had ganged up on me and won out. I held my cane in one hand and Malone's leash in the other. Nolan wasn't a fan of leashes, and I couldn't blame the poor guy. He kept close by me, though, herding me like a sheep dog so I could feel his coat against my leg. I was hemmed in on all sides, which, after all I'd been through, made me feel protected instead of claustrophobic.

I listened to Malone and Nolan speak to each other in their minds, marveling that they could do such a thing. The other healers couldn't hear each other, but I could hear their individual thoughts. What a difference it would make if they could've had their own community of perfect communication. I guessed Malone and Nolan could hear each other either because of the pack mind thing, or because they were twins. Either way, I loved listening to them catalog the different smells, and report back to me the innocuous things that meant to them. None of the things they were labeling meant much to me until they both stopped abruptly, and my knees bumped into Malone's hindquarters. *"No. We'll take another way,"* he insisted. *"This one stinks like sulphur and something sweet. Treats? Chocolates?"*

Nolan pressed his side to me, making sure I didn't move forward a single inch. *"Small tracks, but deep shoeprints. I don't like this. There's nothing like tha around these parts. Stay close, your majesty."*

I bent over and kissed the top of Nolan's head. "For the last time, it's just Rosie. Any guesses as to what we're dealing with?"

Nolan burrowed into my touch, nearly purring with the high of being loved on.

Malone answered for his brother once Nolan started drooling. *"Not a clue, which is the worst part. If we knew what this was, we could make a plan, but seeing as we don't, I'm not comfortable risking ye like tha."*

"Fair enough. I trust you to know the area better than I do." I held up my hand, hoping that the rest of the guys were listening. "Malone and Nolan are seeing weird tracks, and are smelling something funky. They don't trust this path, so we're taking a different route to the footbridge. That cool?"

"What's the smell?" Mad asked, sniffing the air. I listened to his nose test the environment, and then heard him kneel down and smell the ground himself. "I noticed these tracks a while back, but I didn't think it was anything other than a fat lady in tiny heels. But tha's foul. Rotting eggs and... is tha treacle?" He made a noise of disgust, as if even smelling sugar was offensive to him. Dude was going to get a birthday cake the size of his head one day, just so he could try sugar to see if he liked it.

The others got down on their knees to smell the stink in the snow. I had no such desire. Instead, I took the opportunity to crouch down so I could kiss Malone and Nolan on their snouts, scratch behind their ears, and shower them with affection. "It's so much easier to get around with you guys. Thank you. I'd be totally lost out here without you both. Sorry I got kidnapped and had to leave you so soon. I didn't mean to stick you in Avalon and ditch you there. Was Lot good to you?"

"*Aye. Duke Lot's grand. Knighted us and everything, so we could look after ye in a more official capacity.*"

"Oh, wow! Sir Malone and Sir Nolan. That's gotta be something to brag about when you go home."

Malone was firm. "*We won't be going home until ye leave Faîte. And if there might be danger in Common, we'll brave it and go with ye there.*"

I frowned, unsure what to make of this. "I'm not gonna lie, I totally need the extra help these days, but I didn't rescue you just to enslave you. You belong with your family."

"*We're your knights,*" Malone insisted, making me miss Remy. My healer was still out trying to rally the Phare Dullahan, so they could round up some Werewolves for me to heal. Malone nuzzled into my hand. "*We belong wherever ye go. We'd be dead if it weren't for ye, and tha's after all the killing we were setting out to do. Ye saved loads of people by curing us. We aren't leaving your side until you've restored all the Werewolves who need ye.*"

"*Helping ye is helping them. We won't abandon our countrymen.*" Nolan licked my cheek, and then nuzzled my face to warm it. "*Her skin is cold. Closer, Malone.*"

They inched closer, pressing in on both sides as they ground the tops of their heads into me with unconcealed affection. Kindness came easier with animals, I'd found. Even ones that were still human underneath it all. "I don't deserve you guys."

Lugh rose from sniffing the snow and crunched

through the wintery scene over to us. I straightened when he crouched beside me, put his hand on my back and spoke low in my ear. "We're leaving this area. I know these tracks. Very carefully, do as I say. Tell the lads ye can't walk no more. We're turning back right now and heading for shelter."

I didn't know why he was telling me this, instead of talking to all of us. The only reason could be that he sensed danger was too near to be discussed. I squeezed his hand and let out a dramatic yawn. "Guys, I'm real sorry, but I'm beat. I don't know if it's the magical surgery, or talking to Malone and Nolan, but I can't do this tonight."

"We've been walking an hour, and you're just telling us this now?" I could practically see Mad's disapproving expression.

"I'm so sorry. My hand feels funny because of the surgery stuff, and I'm afraid if I do anything with it, it might pop clean off again." I cringed at the ridiculous lie, but being that no one in Faîte had ever undergone a limb reattachment operation, they didn't argue with it.

Bastien stood and moved to my other side. I could feel his irritation at Lugh being so near. Lugh still hadn't removed his hand from the middle of my back but kept it there as a source of protection. "Alright, babe. If you need to lie down, that's fine. It was a guess anyway. Haven't seen a single Werewolf this entire time, so it might've been a bust, going all the way there."

Mad didn't understand social cues, or the "dude, be

cool" look I tried to shoot him. "Go on back, then. I'm going to the footbridge to see if I can gut the creature who's causing all the trouble."

Lugh cleared his throat, and I'm hoping used some sort of physical gesture to flag Mad down. "We need ye back at my place."

I reached for Mad, but all I landed on was air. I had no clue where he was standing. "Malone, can you take me to Mad?"

"Aye. Of course."

Malone tugged on the leash and brought me to Madigan, who was in no mood to turn back. "What?" he asked, his signature scowl evident in his tone.

I reached out and placed my hand on his arm, gently pulling on him so I could whisper in his good ear. "Someone's onto us. We have to go back now and plan something else, before it's too late."

Mad paused and leaned in. "Are ye sure?"

"I'm sure I don't want to risk your life over something that can be put off another night. Let's go." I let out another loud yawn. "Sorry, guys. I'm super way tired."

Bastien's hand took up residence on the small of my back, and Mad took up the rear after Lugh sidled up on my left. My wolves led the way, but no sooner had we all gotten on the same page, did a twig overhead snap, and Lugh shout for us to all run.

Madigan didn't wait for me to chuff along through the

snow that went up to the middle of my shins. He came up from behind and scooped me in his arms, not willing to take a chance on my unsteady feet. The three men charged through the snow, following my wolves, who howled for anyone nearby to save themselves.

17

PETER PAN AND WENDY

*M*adigan never ceased to amaze me. It was his unswerving focus on whatever task he set his mind to that made him unstoppable. I clung to his neck with one arm, and kept my telescoped cane tight to my chest with the other. Though it did nothing to actually shut out the world's chaos, I closed my eyes, fearing the unknown.

"I can still see you," a deep, male voice echoed in my mind. He had a heavy French accent, and a malicious delight in his tone. The reverberations and the calm cadence told me the phantom dude wasn't fussed that we were fleeing. He either didn't want us, or already had us, and our flight was laughable to him.

A shudder ran through my body, but stranger was the growl and shudder that simultaneously ran through Mad, as well. "Did anyone else hear tha?"

"Don't answer the voice, whatever ye do!" Lugh shouted. "Don't talk back to him. It's the Nain Rouge. Once he's got ye, he'll never let ye go!"

"Nolan, run closer to me. I don't want nothing aiming for ye."

"Aye, brother. I've got your back. Ye can lead the way."

Bastien was frantic. "He's in my head! He's saying there's a way to cure Rosie. I have to go to the main city in Éireland to find the Curcuma Longum plant. Is he telling the truth? Is there a chance there's a cure for her blindness?"

Lugh was adamant as his boots pounded through the snow. "We've got Kerdik, Bastien. If a plant could heal her, we can just ask him for it. The Nain gets off on chaos. He wants to take everything good about Faîte and tear it to pieces. Anything he says, put it out of your head. And whatever ye do, don't answer him!"

"You're sure?"

"I'm sure. I was alive before the Nain was captured. He's telling me to shoot an arrow through the wolves right now, because one of them's a spy for Dother."

Both my wolves howled their indignation at being slandered so maliciously. *"We've done no such thing! We gave up everything for Rosie, so she could free Éireland from the Were curse."*

I hurried to assure them that I knew who they were. "I know, guys. I know you're not spies. That's ridiculous."

"Link's not dead," Mad chanted to himself. "Link's just fine. Link's safe and sound with his Quinn. Link's grand."

"Link is alright," I confirmed. "He's probably off telling ridiculous jokes and charming the pants off of Quinn right now." The Nain Rouge seemed to be tapping into our grave fears and desires, which made him all the more dangerous. *How does the Nain even know Link's name if he's never met him?* I tried not to freak out at the mind-reading, but breathe deeply while Mad ran with me in his arms through the snow.

"Aye. Say it again," Mad requested, and I knew the Nain Rouge was getting under his skin.

"Faster!" Lugh urged us. "Run until we can't hear him anymore. He's... It's all lies!" Lugh shouted, as if telling himself along with us.

"I know who your grandmother was. I know what she did. I know what you are," the deep voice said, his heavy French cadence creeping into my psyche like a spider. My spine tingled at his words that held an ominous note I didn't understand. *"I know the true reason they follow you."*

My eyebrows furrowed in confusion, not anger, which the rest of the party seemed to be steeped in. I kept my lips buttoned shut, since this didn't really seem to be the time for a genealogy conversation. I'd never thought to ask about my grandparents; I assumed they were dead, and that was that. Lane never ever talked about her parents.

Bastien was livid at whatever the Nain Rouge was whispering in his ear. "I've had it! This little pest dies tonight!"

Lugh was firm. "No! We don't have the means to destroy him. The only ones who can are the immortals. Prim, page Cailleach and tell her we've got the Nain hot on our heels."

I scolded myself with a giant "duh" for not thinking to do that myself, and pressed my hand to my chest, chanting the Queen of Winter's name three times. It didn't take more than ten of Mad's long strides before I heard Cailleach's voice calling my name in the ever-present darkness. "Rosie, what is it?"

"It's the Nain Rouge! He's in our heads, Callie!" I shouted over Mad's shoulder. He didn't slow, and neither did anyone else, it seemed.

"Run, girl! Faster! Don't answer him, and don't look back. I'll take care of things from here. Go!"

I clung to Mad, feeling terrible for making him carry me while he sprinted. I was a great runner, too, which was the sucky part about being carried. But running through the snow blind wasn't something I could keep pace with the others through. I willed my weight to vanish, thinking thin thoughts in hopes that might somehow help Mad carry me without keeling over.

They ran, it seemed, forever. I heard Malone and Nolan silently encouraging each other, fighting through the violent images they endured of their sister, her mangled and bloody body at the bottom of a river. I wanted to bear the pain for them, but it was then the Nain tired of taunting them and went after me instead.

"You should know better than to run from me. I know who you are. I know what sorcery you use to rope the men in your life into following you. Lugh could tell you all about it."

I scrunched my nose, but kept my lips pressed together. I couldn't guess what the Nain was talking about. My most impressive ability to date was the Compass thing, the unknown languages thing, and flight, I guess, though that was only in my dreamland so far.

The light dinged in my head. "Mad, stop! I can get there myself. You can't keep going like this."

"Are ye sure? Hold my hand, at least." He set me down, too relieved not to have to carry me anymore to protest.

"No need. I can get there myself. I've got my Compass." I ran alongside him, feeling Bastien on my other side. I took a few breaths, recalling the lessons Dub had taught me. I crossed my fingers and prayed those instructions would hold true in real life, and not just in my dream world.

I took in a deep breath and focused on the soles of my feet. I felt the snow up to the middle of my shins, but slowly it only went to my ankles as my feet heated up. I thrilled at the levitation, wanting to shout in victory that finally I wasn't the weak link. I could handle myself and get where I needed to go without a man, without a guide, and without a cane.

Bastien shouted his fear when my feet left the snow altogether. I levitated between them, not wanting to accidentally bang into a tree on the way. I figured if I could stay between the two mammoth men, I wouldn't run that risk. "Rosie, what are you doing? How are you doing that? Make it stop!"

Lugh gasped, and then let out a loud, triumphant laugh. "It's coming back! The magic's coming back to Éireland!" He howled his happiness at the moon like a true frat guy. "Fly, Prim! I'm right behind ye!"

I shrieked when Lugh's arm coiled around my waist, scooping me to his side as we floated higher and higher.

"Put my wife down!" Bastien shouted, his anger sounding more territorial than fearful for my safety.

"She's alright, Bastien. I'll get her faster to the cabin this way. It's safer, yeah?"

Bastien let out a growl of fury at the solid logic.

"Honey, it's alright. I promise, I'm okay." I squeezed Lugh. "Let's stay where he can see me, so he doesn't flip out."

"It's safer to get ye away from the Nain Rouge as quick as we can." Then to Bastien, he shouted, "Do ye trust her, Bastien? We have to get her out now. Kerdik would murder me too many times over if I made off with your lady."

"Fine, go!" Bastien cried out in something that sounded like defeat.

"So, Peter Pan, you can fly, too?" I asked, shocked. Even though I could make it on my own, I clung to him, just in case there was a tree or something.

"Aye, Wendy. Used to be able to, just like the others who were born with too much magic. I just didn't realize we could've been flying, now tha the magic's back in the land. I think everyone assumed it was gone for good. After all but me were destroyed of the Gancanagh race, not too many are powerful enough to fly."

I grinned that I'd found a way to not be helpless. "Dub taught me how in my dreams. I took a shot and hoped it would work here. Lucky timing, I guess."

Lugh tilted us forward to lessen the wind resistance. He held me tight, though it wasn't out of worry. He was happy, and I'd been the one to add to his smile. "Ye made me fly, Prim. All this time, I never knew. I needed someone to show me the magic again."

I smirked at him, tucking myself into his embrace as we left the others behind. "Anytime, friend."

18

GOOD GOLLY, MISS MOLLY

We reached the cabin long before anyone else, but Lugh was hesitant to go inside. "Something's not right. Go in and wait for me there. I'm going to check the grounds."

I unfolded my cane when I stepped into the cabin and felt my way along the wall, anchoring myself there as I skirted the perimeter of the living room. I moved down the hallway, hoping to find an out of the way place to warm up and lay low while Lugh assessed the threat. I found my way to the bedroom I was pretty sure I'd been given refuge in, and plastered my back to the wall, exhaling all my anxiety. "Finally." The Nain Rouge's voice disappeared a while back, but I kept waiting to hear it again – part of me not wanting to, but the other part needing to hear more of the puzzle he'd dumped out all over the floor of my psyche. I needed more information about my grandparents.

I frowned as I felt around for the bed, wondering why it was that I had mostly male friends in Faîte. I'd initially written it off as the population stilt – with their being two men to every one woman. Still, the Nain's words taunted me.

My hand landed down on the edge of the mattress, but jumped back when I heard a woman say, "Wow, I guess ye really are blind."

"What the crap, dude? Who are you? Does Lugh know you're in here?"

"He'll be happy I've come to see him."

My nose scrunched in confusion. "Molly? Is that you, girl? Seriously, what are you doing here?"

"Lugh wanted me to come, I'm sure of it. You're trying to get in his bed, aren't ye?"

"Um, no. Dude, I'm pretty sure this is my bed. Lugh's is the first one on the right, down the hall."

She sounded like she was frowning. "What? Oh, bollocks. See tha ye leave us to our privacy, then. I'll wait for him in his room."

As Molly shifted off the bed, she gave me a hard shove, positioning her leg behind me, so I fell backwards onto my butt. It stung my pride worse than anything else, but I fought to keep my cool. I gritted my teeth to keep from spouting something childishly acerbic at her. I didn't want to fight her, mostly because I didn't feel like I totally understood the situation.

Had Lugh really invited a girl back to his place who'd

been part of the lynching mob that wanted me thrown out of the bar? She'd accused me of biting her after we'd had our totally cool girl chat. I'd even gotten her a dance with Lugh, who was supposedly the hottest guy there. Then when the mob turned on me, she turned, and chimed in every chance she could to get me thrown out. I stayed down, listening to her bare feet pad out of the room, and move down the hall to Lugh's bedroom.

When the front door opened, Lugh's voice carried through the cabin. "Prim, are ye alright in here? I don't know where they came from, but there are footprints outside."

I frowned, planting my hands on the floor behind me. "Well, your date's waiting in your room, so I'm guessing those tracks came from her."

Right on cue, Molly's syrupy voice wafted from Lugh's bedroom. "Oh, lover! I've come to warm ye up on this cold, cold night."

I paused at the confusion and discomfort in Lugh's voice. "Uh, what? Who are ye, and what are ye doing in my house? Get out here and show yourself!" After the door creaked open, he exclaimed an appalled, "Jays, woman! Put some clothes on! What are ye doing, roaming about my house stark raving naked? How did ye even get in?"

"Ye didn't lock the door all tha tight. Anyone who knows how to pick a lock could wander on in. I thought ye might want to finish tha dance before the she-Vamp bewitched ye and turned your head in her direction."

"You're from the pub? We danced?"

"Ye don't remember?" She sounded hurt, but then her voice turned coy. "Get on tha bed, so I can punish ye for forgetting me. Ye won't make tha mistake again."

Lugh exhaled, and I could tell he was sad when he spoke again. "Listen, you're probably a very fine lass, but ye wouldn't be doing this if *I* hadn't bewitched *ye*. Not Prim. Me. I must've sweat on ye while we were dancing. I'm Gancanagh. Ye don't want me. Not as much as ye think ye do, anyway."

I leaned forward on the floor and palmed my forehead. Lugh was Gancanagh, which, in the limited explanation he'd given me, meant that his sweat excreted a poison that made women crave him in unquenchable ways. I'd pushed him on her to dance so she could have her moment with the hot guy. It explained why she'd turned so nasty to me in the pub after their dance. I'd done this to her. Lugh hadn't wanted to dance with her, but I'd pushed him to have fun. It was reckless of me, and now he was getting *Fatal Attraction*ed.

"I do want ye. It's all I want. Touch me, Lugh. The way ye didn't hesitate to kill the bloke when he knocked tha Vampire scum ye were with? It gave me the shivers. Haven't ye ever looked at someone and gotten the shivers, Cross Shot?"

"Aye, but tha's not what this is. And I killed tha lad because tha's the law. If we don't have the unbreakable code of the Untouchables, we have nothing as a society."

"My Da told me all kinds of stories about ye when I was a girl. Cross Shot, who never misses. Doesn't look back after he takes his enemy down." I heard her voice turn husky. "I pictured ye defending my honor like tha. Murdering a lad in cold blood for me. It took some time, but I managed to sneak away from my parents. I'm here now. We can be together."

"Put on your clothes, lass. I'll not have this conversation with ye when ye don't have your knickers on."

"Ye don't like what ye see?"

I blanched, wishing I could vanish into thin air just to avoid being a fly on the wall to this awful conversation. It felt like a giant step back for women everywhere.

"I think long pants are sexy," Lugh replied, switching his tone to a softer, more seductive one. "I think shirts are simply ravishing. Makes me imagine what it'll be like when I tear it off a woman. Ye went ahead and stole all the fun from me. Get on in there and get dressed."

"Aye, love. I'll give ye all sorts of things to imagine." She skipped down the hall to my room. I guessed that she must've left her clothes in here. Her saccharine voice dropped to unveiled disgust when she entered and started putting on her clothes. I sat on the bed with my head down, trying to appear submissive, so as not to invoke a fight with someone so clearly unbalanced. "What are ye still doing here? He'll never marry ye. I'm the lady of the house now, so ye might as well leave us."

I didn't bother to answer, because I learned long ago

that you can't argue with crazy and expect to have a rational outcome. I slowly stood, keeping my head down in hopes she'd be bored with me, and Lugh could deal with her.

"It's a good thing you're blind, otherwise you'd see me in all my glory, and you'd know there's no chance for ye. Flaunting your bosom in the pub like tha? Shameful! Lugh likes his women demure in public. Now, get out of here."

When Molly smacked me upside the head, I tried not to turn on my raging pit bull persona. I breathed through my nose and kept my cool until Molly slapped me across the face. I let out a tiny bleat of shock at being so thoroughly insulted. There's something about that demeaning act that felt like the gauntlet had been thrown. "Uh, Lugh? A little help in here?"

Lugh was already trotting toward us, making his way to my side. He moved my hand from my face and hissed. "Are ye alright, Prim?"

"I'm fine. Just deal with your situation before I lose my cool."

"I don't like when ye touch her," Molly warned. "I came here to marry ye, Lugh. I'll not tolerate your hands on another woman."

"Listen, Prim's got nothing to do with this situation. She's married, remember? You're bewitched, lass. Ye don't want me. If ye can outlast the poison, you'll regret this day very much. I don't want tha. I don't want ye to be ashamed of taking your clothes off for a man who doesn't know ye. I'm sure you're a lovely person. You'll meet a lad someday who knows ye, and who invites ye into his house. Ye won't have to break into the right lad's home."

"It's her," Molly sneered. "She's in your head. I saw it back at the pub, and I still see she's got her hooks into ye. I've come to set ye free, Lugh! Don't ye see tha? Don't ye see tha I've left my family, my village, my friends and everyone just to rescue ye?"

"I don't need rescuing! It's... This is hopeless."

She moved over to the corner of the room and fidgeted with whatever was on the chair there. "I can fix it, though. I can save ye, sweetheart."

"What are ye thinking of doing with tha knife, woman?" His voice sounded resigned, as if he already knew, and there was no stopping it. "Put it down, now."

I scrambled away and backed up until my butt hit the wall, unsure how to defend myself against a girl I didn't truly want to hurt. "Careful," I warned him, hoping he was as good at stopping knives as he was at murdering people with them.

"Come to my bedroom," Lugh cooed to her. "Let's get better acquainted and leave Prim to her married lady activities. There's nothing I'd like more than to spend some time with ye. There's so much I don't know."

"With me, ye can have everything. Every single thing. Just name it."

"I want your knife. It unnerves me to make love to a

woman who's holding a blade like tha. Give it to me, and I'll take ye to my room."

"Of course!"

She breezed past me, and before Lugh followed her, he whispered in my ear, "Lock the door."

19

WHY I FOUND TWO LOVES

Lugh came back to my room ten minutes later, his steps heavy with duty instead of his spritely "The world could never bog me down; I'm a rock star" jaunt. "Tha should buy us a little time."

"Where is she?"

"Asleep in my bed. I drugged her. Had to," he explained when I gasped my indignation. "Ye don't understand, Prim. Once a lass has been poisoned by my sweat, she'll stop at nothing. Everything around us is a threat she thinks is keeping us apart. Turns even the sweetest lass into a psycho. She's knocked out for her own good – for your own good, really. She thought we were…"

I grimaced. "Gross."

Lugh balked at me. "Ye could do a lot worse."

"Dude, you're like, super old."

I felt the whoosh of Lugh talking with his hands.

"Kerdik's eternal! I'm not older than him. I'm only sixty-two, if ye remember."

"Oh, I totally thought you were like, ninety or something. Either way, Molly can have you."

I heard him slap his forehead in revelation. "Molly! Tha's her name. I couldn't remember, and I was afraid she might try and stab me if I asked."

"So, does the mojo wear off eventually? How long is she going to be like this?"

"Depends on how much sweat she absorbed into her skin. Most times it's a few months – just long enough for the psychosis to set in deep, and for her to ruin her life so there's nothing to go back to."

"Oh, jeez. That's terrible. Is there anything I can do?"

"Nah. Kerdik usually takes care of stuff like this for me. I feel bad bothering him when he's off doing important stuff, like he is now. But there's no other way. Hopefully she sleeps until he gets here. Would ye mind paging him for me?"

"Sure." I pressed my palm to my chest and said Kerdik's name three times. When he didn't immediately appear, I realized how spoiled I'd become, expecting a man to appear at my side when I summoned him.

"He's busy, then," Lugh observed. "When I was out with him and ye paged, he was panicked if he couldn't get to ye in the first five seconds. He'd start mumbling stuff like, 'Don't let it happen to her again!' He'd abandon whatever we were doing and port to your side."

I squinted at Lugh. "You got a point there, chief?"

"Ye sure broke in the wildest stallion quick, is all."

I rolled my shoulders back, affronted. "Dude, you're the one who's got a chick in his bed who's coocoo for your Cocoa Puffs. I didn't break Kerdik. He does what he likes. You, of all people, should know that."

"It was a compliment, Prim."

"It felt like an insinuation." I lowered my voice, though no one was around to hear us. "You're old, right? So you might know stuff about Avalon before I was born."

"Aye. A little. I lived in Éireland, though, so I'm not sure how useful I might be on the subject. And I'm not old. If I was aging, I wouldn't even have all tha many wrinkles yet."

"Just something the Nain Rouge whispered in my ear."

"It was lies," Lugh ruled.

"You don't even know what he said!"

"I don't need to. His only mission is to drum up chaos. It was a lie, whatever he told ye. Best put it out of your mind."

"Please, Lugh. I need to know. What can you tell me about my grandparents?"

Lugh stopped blowing me off, and his reply came back confused. "Your grandparents? Morgan le Fae's parents, or King Urien's?"

"Either set, I guess."

"Hmm. Don't know why I asked ye tha. I don't know much about either side. I think Morgan le Fae's mammy's name was Diana or something like tha. She was the ruler of Avalon before the sisters split Avalon into provinces. I don't remember your grandda's name, but there was some kind of controversy about how he landed Diana. She was a prize piece, ye understand, plus powerful on top of tha, and the bloke was... very average. He grew on the people, but she had suitors for miles, and she chose him who had no noble breeding, wasn't anything to look at, and hadn't been properly educated. I think he was a farmer or something like tha."

It was all the confirmation I needed. "So there's a chance my grandfather was Gancanagh?"

Lugh sounded confused. "I mean, there's a chance anyone could be tha, I guess. I was only a lad back then, so I couldn't tell ye for certain."

I reached out and felt Lugh's shoulder, climbing my way up his neck so I could feel the curves of his face. I needed to gauge his reaction, which was difficult to do with hearing alone. He leaned in, so I could touch him as I pleased. "Tell me the truth, Lugh. If my grandfather was Gancanagh, could he have passed that down? Is it a genetic trait?"

"Aye, but he only had daughters. A rare thing for a family to have nine daughters and no sons. They were revered for tha. It used to be one of the old blessings people would say at weddings. 'May ye have as many daughters as the Queen of Avalon.'"

"What if you're wrong? What if my grandpa found a way to pass down his genetics to my moms and my aunts?"

The pieces slowly began to slide together as I puzzled through it all aloud. "Don't you think it's a little strange that people followed Morgan as long as they did? That no matter how evil she got, or what great options the dukes presented with their land, the people still flocked to her?"

"No more odd tha people flocked to Hitler, I guess. Some people just want to be led. They want to pass off their problems onto someone else, not caring how they solve them, so long as nothing harrowing is on their own plate anymore."

I considered his logic. "I guess. Don't you think it's strange that I'm an outsider here, yet I managed to marry an Untouchable?"

"No. Tha part makes perfect sense. Untouchables are outsiders. They don't fit in anywhere. Tha lass Link settled down with? His mate? From what I understand, she's an outsider in the Faire Séparer Clan. It would be strange to me if ye were a regular citizen of Avalon, and ye managed to hook an Untouchable. But being tha you're an outlier, tha makes sense."

"Maybe." I could feel Lugh's breath on my nose, but I didn't step back. If anyone saw us with my hands on his cheeks and him standing so close, they would get the wrong idea. "What about Kerdik?"

"What about him, now?"

"Don't you think it's weird that we hooked up? That he gave me this ring the first day he met me as an adult? That he lets me call him whenever? I'm no one, and he's this super powerful being. I'm not throwing a pity party here; I'm legitimately asking, why me? Doesn't it seem... Something's fishy!"

"Oh, Prim. Tha ye have to ask tha shows me how little ye understand of the world, and of men."

I frowned at his assessment. "Call me a dummy all you want, but I know when something's off. I'm telling you, I think I'm part Gancanagh! It's in my blood, Lugh. There's no other explanation why I've got Bastien and Kerdik. And Mad and Link? They call me their wife! Link murdered a whole battalion when some of Morgan's soldiers molested me."

"They did *what* now?"

I paused for a beat, my hands freezing on his cheeks. "Sorry, I assumed Kerdik told you what happened. I got captured, and the soldiers wanted to have a little fun. Kerdik and Link showed up after I paged Kerdik, and the two of them got me my clothes back and cleaned house."

"No, he never told me any of tha. But it makes more sense now, I guess. Tha must be why he loses his mind when ye page him. Probably afraid something like tha's happening again."

"But Kerdik's not exactly known for his bleeding heart. Why does he care if I'm in danger?"

"Because he loves ye."

I rolled my eyes. "I'm not looking for Hallmark answers here. I need to know if it's real, or if Molly was right. Do I bewitch people? Is that what's been happening? Because I gotta tell you, I never even had a date before I came to Avalon."

Lugh smirked. "Didn't ye tell me ye used to have a hump and all tha? Maybe the reasons aren't as magical as you're thinking. As for Bastien, I don't know the bloke, but he seems to genuinely love ye. Devoted husband, if ever I saw one. Ye break a nail, and he's practically tearing down trees to build ye a nail file."

"But he didn't use to be like that. We took forever to get together."

"Ah, then it can't be Gancanagh magic. Tha's instant. And he's got tha Vampire's mate addiction now to add to his hunger for ye." Lugh wrapped his arms around me to soothe my worries. "Don't listen to the Nain Rouge. He's a pest who wants ye all turned around. He wants to upset your marriage. He needs ye to run away from Kerdik, who can protect ye. Women can't be Gancanagh. It's never happened, Prim. Not genetically possible."

I gave up my fight for the moment and leaned my temple to Lugh's firm shoulder. He was leaner than Bastien, with a body that seemed more agile than it was ready to knock down walls with his bare fists. "So much of it makes sense, though. What if my whole life isn't real? What if I accidentally magicked it into being? Am I holding them hostage?"

"You're doing no such thing. They wouldn't leave your side if ye pushed them out the front door."

Lugh sifted his fingers through mine and held my arm

out to the side. He started humming as his feet began to move in a slow box step. It took a few false starts, but once he tightened his grip around my hips, mashing my pelvis to his, we moved in-sync around the bedroom. I don't know how he got me to dance again, but something in me actually needed the sweetness of a gesture that simple. I needed a touch of beauty to decorate the grim uncertainty.

"I'll get to the bottom of your heritage as soon as all of this is put to rest. If your grandda was Gancanagh, tha's good news for us."

"Us? What do you mean?"

"Unless I'm in Common, where my magic is muted, I'm a danger to women. I can't have female friends in Faîte. One wrong move, and their life is ruined by some sick fascination they can't curb. But if you've got Gancanagh in ye, then I can sweat all over ye, and it won't do a thing."

"Please put that in a Christmas card to me. 'I'm so glad I can sweat all over you. Let's be friends.'"

Lugh chuckled as he took wider turns, now that I'd stopped stepping on his feet. "I was worried I might've sweat on ye in the pub, but then Kerdik showed up, and ye could barely remember my name."

I scrunched my nose. "Hmm. Boo? Stu? Poo, is it?"

We shared a small chuckle. "Now we don't have to worry about tha. I'm positive I sweat on ye when I was shielding ye from the Weres. I didn't know what to make of it when ye weren't infatuated." I could hear his grin. "Ye have no idea how careful I have to be. To have a woman I can actually be friends with in Faîte? It's grand, Prim. Grander than I imagined. You're not Gancanagh, but somehow ye might be immune to my poison. A luckier lad there never was than me right now."

I smirked at his cuteness. "I like having you around, too, Lugh."

"And as far as ye worrying about Bastien and Kerdik wanting ye for any reason other than who ye are, I can't imagine anything more ridiculous. Any man can clearly see it's them who landed the prize, not the other way around."

I let his sweet words fill me with a fuzzy warmth that made my insides glow and purr. "Thanks, man. You're a good guy."

"Don't go spreading tha around. I've got a rock star bad boy image to protect."

I contented myself to snuggle into Lugh's affection, both of us finding something rare in Faîte – a friend who was worth saving a dance for.

20

WHEN BASTIEN'S AFRAID

*J*umped away from Lugh when the door banged open, worried that some bad guy had busted inside. Lugh tucked my body behind his with careful, agile movements that told me he would handle whoever it was.

"Daisy?"

My heart rose in my breast at the sound of my guy coming home safe. "Bastien, we're in here!"

Lugh dropped his protective stance and opened the bedroom door. "Cheers. Everyone made it back alright, then?"

Bastien was in no mood. "You don't shut yourself in a room alone with my wife. I don't care if Kerdik vouched for you."

Lugh sounded bored. "Something tells me I might be cordially uninvited to the gingerbread house contests this

Christmas, Prim. I was in there with her because she was attacked, and I thought her husband would want her as safe as possible."

"Attacked? Where? In the air?"

Lugh filled Bastien in on the Sleeping Beauty in the next room. "Don't worry. Kerdik will take care of the mess when he gets here."

Bastien moved to stand in front of me, but he didn't hug me, which felt off. I guessed he was pissed about something. "Where did you learn to fly? And how is it you discovered magic like that, but didn't think to tell me? I'm supposed to be your *Guardien*. I think I ought to know if my charge is going to start shooting into the sky."

I explained my brief lessons with Dub. "I didn't think it would translate into real life, and I learned it after I was already kidnapped. It's hard to tell what's a dream in there, and what holds true out here. I took a shot, which I'm sure Mad's grateful for. I can't imagine he'd want to haul me around during that whole run."

"You should've told me. I don't like when you keep secrets, because it's always something big like this. It's a bomb that gets dropped on my head in the times I'm least prepared for it. We're running, and boom! My wife's flying through the air."

"Okay, dude. I'm sorry. I didn't mean to scare you."

"Well, I was scared."

"I know. You always turn pissy when you're afraid."

This was clearly the wrong thing to say. "I'll pretend

you didn't say that. I was scared because if something happened to you up there, I couldn't do anything to save you. I can't block an arrow that's aimed at you if you're higher than the trees! And you're afraid of heights!"

"Are you accusing me of something? Because it sure sounds like you are. I can't actually see how high up I get. Lugh guided me so I didn't bash my head on any branches. I'm safe. You're safe. It's all fine. You know, when you get overprotective, you yell like a child."

"You make me crazy!"

"Yeah? Well, you make me laugh with all this nonsense. I made the right call, and you know it. Deal with your emotions, dude. Don't take it out on me."

I was grateful to hear Lugh making his way down the hall to greet Madigan, Nolan and Malone, though I heard him chuckling at our fight as he left us.

Bastien lowered his voice to a controlled seethe. "You can't disappear like that ever again. Don't you get how crazy I've been without you? Whenever we have to separate, I hate every day of it. We're in Faîte together, no matter what. You and I aren't splitting up again, understand?"

I saluted him just to be a jerk. "Sir, yes sir!"

"And I don't like that Lugh character sniffing around you."

"You're paranoid. Lugh's way old, and he's my friend – which is something I need here. He had my back when I got ganged up on in that pub. He's never tried anything in all the time we've spent together. He knows I'm super married, so don't make a big thing out of it. Don't you want to spend our time together not talking about another dude?"

"I want to not worry when you're away from me."

"What's the likelihood of that happening?"

Bastien slumped, curling his arms around me. "Until Dother's locked away? Slim to none."

I leaned up and planted a kiss in the sensitive spot on his neck. "I'm here, and I'm totally safe. Lugh might as well be a girl, with how much heat there isn't between us. You've got your arms around your wife, and that bed over there is begging to be broken in again. What do you say, chief? You seem like you could use a little time to unwind."

He was sweaty from his run, even through his coat, which he hadn't taken off yet. I unbuttoned the front, reaching inside to run my fingers up and down the hard planes of his torso. My nails snuck under his sweat-soaked shirt, dancing along the equator of his waist just to make his toned belly dance for me.

"I'm still mad at you," he reminded us, but I could smell an easy takedown.

I leaned up on my toes to whisper in his ear as I unbuttoned his jeans. "Then I think you should punish me."

Bastien groaned, not letting another second go to waste. He shed his coat, his shirt, his boots and socks, and barely had the patience for me to fiddle with the extraction of his pants. He swung the bedroom door shut, ignoring

Lugh's warning that we should pack up and leave soon. I grinned when my husband all but threw me onto the mattress, arresting my clothes in record time. "We're done fighting our way through this world separately," he growled in a tone that made it clear there would be no other way. "We belong together, Daisy." His large hands made quick work of pressing all the right buttons. He was unpolished and calloused, but that's what I liked about him. Whenever he was scared, the lovemaking was rough and passionate – just how I liked it.

Just how we needed it.

21

WHISPERS OF LIES

"Do we even know where we're going?" Bastien asked as he hoisted my bag and his over his shoulder.

Malone was of the same mind as Bastien. *"I don't like the idea of leaving with no destination agreed on."*

"We can't risk the Nain finding us here. It's not exactly a secret tha I own this land. If he knows who I am, then he'll come this way and try to get in our heads again."

"What about our village? We can hide out with our parents until it all blows over," Nolan suggested, and I relayed the message to the group.

I could tell Lugh was trying to iron the irritation from his response. "There is no blowing over for the Nain. There's a fire that grows ever larger, until the whole of Éireland is screaming for mercy. Prim seems to be a magnet for danger. Do ye really want to bring tha kind of calamity to your parents' house?"

"Hey!" I said, indignant.

Malone moved toward the hallway. *"Nolan, it's going to be dawn soon. Let's go into the bedroom and change so we don't draw out Master Kerdik's wrath if we're naked in front of Rosie."*

"Aye. Don't leave without us."

"Of course, guys."

Lugh paced the living room as he spoke. "We need a place in the middle of nowhere tha I don't own. The Nain might remember me and know of my other haunts." Lugh was flustered. I could tell he just wanted to get out of here, and figure out the rest later. "He'll come for us if Cailleach can't take him down. When he does, we won't escape quite as easily as we did last time."

I shuddered, wishing I had a little more peace about it all. I kept my hand tight in Bastien's to reassure him that we would be together this time. "So, this Nain Rouge. Pretty bad dude?"

Lugh took it upon himself to be the historian of the group, since he was far older than any of us. "Bad, indeed. He used to specialize in fire, but with everything covered in snow, he's got to get a bit more crafty if he's to let his usual havoc ensue. He's got one goal, Prim: chaos. The more he gets of it, the happier he is. He wants families to turn on each other, nations to implode from the inside out – all of it. If ye answer his voice when he gets in your head, he'll never leave ye alone. He'll stay in ye until ye go mad, and he wins. I want us as far from him as we can get. Ye especially, Prim."

"Why me?"

"Because we've been given double-long lives. Do ye really want to be taunted for the next hundred and fifty years by tha weasel?"

"Yikes. I didn't think about that. Good call. Where are we headed?"

"We can go to my place," Mad offered. "No one will bother us there. It's a day's walk, but if we fly, t'won't be tha difficult."

I held up my free hand. "Wait a second. I don't know how to carry someone while I'm flying. I only just tried it out for the first time in real life with you guys out there."

"I can show ye, Prim. And the Untouchables should be able to fly, once we teach them how. They've got more magic than the average citizen."

A pop and a thud of feet on the floor told me an immortal had joined us. "Kerdik?"

Cailleach's reply met my ears. "Rosie, grand. Just who I needed to see. Quick, darling, I need your help."

"No," Malone ruled, sounding like a father figure more and more. He moved to stand at my other side, and I could feel the brush of his arm against mine, letting me know he wasn't in his wolf form anymore. "I'll not allow it, your majesty. We're leaving, and the queen is coming with us."

My nose scrunched. "*My* help? What could I possibly do that you can't?"

"My cane!" she exclaimed in a mournful tone. It was then that I smelled the waft of smoke billowing out from her gown as she gestured. "I can't open it to summon the Nain Rouge back inside. Kerdik must've done something to it to make it impossible to open again after the fight with Dother and Dian. I'll deal with him later, but for now I need your ring."

I clenched my fist, hoping she didn't mean to take it from me. I didn't care much about the thing, but the more people tried to take it off my hand, the steeper my stubborn nature grew. "The ring stays on my finger."

"Of course. I mean to take ye with me, as well. I need something that can hold the Nain Rouge prisoner. I don't have the time to make myself a new vessel."

"Oh, sure. That's fine. Let's do it. Where is he?"

"No," Lugh ruled. "Ye know tha's too dangerous, Cailleach. He's already been whispering lies in her head."

Her retort was imperious, and I could visualize her body rising with anger at being contradicted. "Know your place, Cross Shot. I've no interest in your opinion. Rosie, it's time. I've put out a few of his fires, but more will be blazing this way soon enough. I need ye to come with me and use your ring."

The scent of the smog on her dress was strong, my nose crinkling to get away from the stench. "Sure thing. Bastien, you want to come, or do you want to stay here?"

He gripped my hand, as if I was a flight risk. "I told you, we're not separating ever again."

"Loyal as a dog, isn't he?"

My head jerked to the sides. "Malone? Nolan? You're in your Fae forms, right? You're not wolves?"

"Aye. The sun's rising, so we're upright again."

"I heard him, then! The Nain Rouge must've followed you here, Callie! He's in my head!"

"We're leaving, then. Go, quick!" Malone ordered, running to the front door to fling it open.

Before I could unfold my cane, one of the windows exploded, sending shards of glass everywhere. Nolan tackled me backward into the hallway, and then pressed me onto the ground, shielding me with his body as the glass shot out at us, and the winter wind gusted inside.

Nolan's body was tensed atop mine, his youthful trepidation of the fight making his muscles clench as he held his body taut. "Easy, my queen. I've got ye covered."

"But no one's covering you!" I retorted, furious that he thought my life was more important than his own.

It was at that moment another blast echoed through the house, shaking the walls and vibrating the floor beneath me. Heat started to crackle down the hall in the living room. I heard Nolan's yelp of pain, and then went temporarily deaf when another boom ripped through the house, this time accompanied by crackles of fire.

I gritted my teeth against the voice that wafted through my mind. *"You've enslaved him long enough, Gancanagh. I'll be the one to set your loyal dog free."*

Something hit Nolan, and he cried out before he

collapsed atop me, his body tensing once more before his muscles released with a heavy gust. I could tell he was saying something, but I couldn't hear a thing, save for the Nain Rouge taunting me with a steady stream of, *"Wherever you go, I'll find you."*

22

HE LOVED YOU, AND IT KILLED HIM

couldn't rouse Nolan, no matter how much I tried. He was also heavy as a tank, so I couldn't get him off of me, either. I couldn't hear anything except the Nain Rouge with his low, velvety French accent murmuring sour nothings in my ear. *"You killed him. He loved you, and it killed him."*

I screamed out, hoping someone could help me revive Nolan. Sweet Nolan, who wanted to marry a milkmaid and smoke his pipe out on his porch. He wanted the simplest things in life, but I'd made it so he couldn't have any of it. My hand snuck up and tested his pulse, hoping that in the madness, I would feel something stirring beneath my fingertips. This was Montel all over again. He'd befriended me, had fought to keep me safe, and paid for my life with his own against the Sluagh. There was Demi, who'd been killed because I loved him. I carried that guilt with me, and prayed that Nolan's name wouldn't be added to the list of people who had given everything because they believed I needed to be spared.

For what? Apart from my birthright, and my stupid ring that could've gone on anyone's finger, I was ordinary – perhaps painfully so. I hadn't earned those things. I was the fake kind of special, and yet people were throwing themselves in front of bullets to save me because they thought I meant something to Faîte.

I wanted to mean something to Faîte. I wanted to put an end to the terror and set order back again. I wanted *Attelage* Vamps to be able to get a drink at a bar without being segregated or thrown completely out. I wanted the provinces to get along, and for the Sons of Carman to leave us all the crap alone.

I wanted peace, which seemed eons away in the rubble. The chaos had ended for Nolan, but not so much for me.

I snuggled under Nolan's body, planting little kisses on his chin and neck. His blood dribbled across my lips, but I didn't smear it away. His blood was spilling for me, so I licked my lips and took him into my being, hoping I could keep him with me a little while longer.

"Even your father knows the abomination you are. Look at you, feeding off a corpse when you should be fighting me. You're a bigger monster than I, no? But let's see who comes out on top this time."

I wanted to bellow out a ferocious, "What do you want

from me?" but I remained firm in not answering the Nain Rouge.

"Ah, yes. Kerdik's little prize. I had no idea you would be so... average. He locked me up with Carman all those years ago. Do you have any idea what that feels like? To be stuck with that cackling lunatic for decades? If they thought I was twisted before, they have no idea all I can do now."

I chewed on my lower lip, my hands snaking around Nolan's midsection. I tried to rip the shards of glass from his back, in hopes that might somehow bring him back to life. I could hear the fire roaring, but didn't know how to escape with everyone.

"I don't want to risk getting near Kerdik again, but I'll make his life miserable while I have you. Then after you, I'll start in on Cross Shot. After I eat his entrails, I'll hunt down the Great King Urien – Kerdik's last friend. Anyone he's ever cared for, I'll destroy slowly and painfully – starting with you."

I closed my lip through my scream, wishing I could hear anything else. I wanted to warn them all to run, Lugh especially, but I was afraid that if I opened my mouth, I would answer the Nain with a fiery retort.

When a miniature hand gripped my shoulder, I felt sharp claws dig into the flesh there. I wanted to twist away, but again, Nolan protected me. His heavy weight made it impossible for me to wriggle much, which meant the claws didn't tear me to shreds in my fight.

"Now you're mine," the Nain chortled, finally yanking me out from under Nolan and dragging me across the

floor. My back and my butt caught too many shards of glass, and I felt them tearing into me, slicing in small cuts and large gashes.

I twisted in his grip, putting aside the searing pain in my shoulder from his knife-like nails. I felt something important tear in my shoulder, but managed to extract myself from his grip.

It was at that moment Dub decided to throw me a bone and give my sight back to me. I stumbled around as I tried to orient myself in the cabin, hitting my already injured shoulder on the doorframe in the hallway. It was too much for my eyes to take in all at once. One glance out toward the living room told me the others had their hands full with the fire that had claimed the wooden ceiling. Malone was burned on his arm, but that didn't seem to deter his fervor. They were shouting, but I couldn't hear a thing still. I gaped at Bastien, who stabbed his knife through... a Sluagh?

The hooded black figure was unmasked, revealing a decaying face similar to the one I'd seen back in Lane's palace. I bit back my panic at the Fae gone wrong. Sluagh's were born when a wicked Fae died and came back as a malicious spirit. Their mission was to suck out the souls from the living – souls of the good or the bad. They weren't truly alive or dead, but each soul they stole made them stronger. My insides turned cold when Madigan fought wildly against four Sluaghs, who were determined to make a meal out of him.

The Nain spoke in my head, bringing my focus back to him. *"I'm going to tear you apart, cook you over my fire and eat you, bite by bite, until Kerdik will only have your hair to bury."*

Of all the hubbub around me, the Nain Rouge was the thing that caught me the most by surprise. I'd been expecting an overlarge red man to be the one taunting my thoughts, but dude barely cleared three feet tall. He had a red body, clad only in black trousers and suspenders, with no shirt beneath. His black hair and villain's beard with one curly, pointy end hanging off his chin made him look comically sinister. I idly wondered if this guy was where Commoners got our drawings of the red devil with a pitchfork.

He smiled at me – an evil expression that invoked more fear in me than a snarl would've. *"It looks like the others are busy with my little distractions. I have more, you know. I could easily fill this place with a dozen more Sluagh. There's something poetic about help being right there, but the day going to ruin anyway. Ah, poetry."*

I guessed the others were just as deaf from the boom as I was, since no one heard me scream for them to get out of the house.

"Aren't you curious about what I told you? About your grandfather, and how you came into such luck? I'll bet if you told Kerdik of my theory, he'd see right through his attraction to you, straight to the truth of why he can't seem to shake such an average Commoner."

I loathed the grandstanding, but it bought me enough

time to gather myself, collecting my bearings while my back burned from the open sores and glass still jutting out of me. I turned and ran down the hall, but didn't make it more than three steps before a ring of fire shot out from Nain like a lasso, wrapping itself around my ankle and dropping me to the ground with a thud. I screamed at the flame's tight hold on me, devouring tender flesh as it climbed up my leg.

Cailleach's gaze darted to me, and without a word, she shot a stream of snow from her palms. The thick, fluffy white cooled my leg, but it also helped to put out the fire, encasing my leg in a freeze no flame could survive.

Only it did survive. The fire danced atop the snow, as if to stick its tongue out at me, proving it was stronger, faster, and could outlast even an immortal. The blaze danced along the snow's packed surface, climbing its way up my leg toward my hip, seeking out new flesh to conquer.

It was then I decided I'd been conquered enough. I did the old stop, drop and roll, which put out the last of the orange flickers that threatened to eat me alive. The Nain laughed in my head, kindling a fury in me he should've run from. Despite my badly burned leg, I stood, crying out at the pain I was determined to walk off.

"Destroy that ring, and I'll never bother you or your friends again. I know Cailleach means to lock me inside."

I don't know how I had the presence of mind to keep my mouth shut and not spew vitriol at him, but I prayed my focus would hold. I held my shoulder and turned toward the others, judging the Sluaghs would be an easier kill than this dude. I ambled toward the living room, moving past Nolan's limp body with a muffled sob, and tried my hand at killing a Sluagh with my bare hands (which I knew wasn't actually possible). I wanted to use my icy blast Cailleach had given me, but I couldn't focus enough to summon any real magic inside of me. I was in rip-tear-kill mode, disoriented and short of breath from the smoke.

I barely set one foot inside the living room before the Nain in my ass tackled me around the waist from behind, knocking us both to the ground. His claws dug into my freshly healed hip, scraping from front to back. He cackled at my pain, which bumped my fury to the number one spot in the litany of things I was feeling in that moment. I rolled over and knocked him across his smug little bearded face, screaming as the shards of glass in my back were lodged deeper. I punched him again because I was pissed. My fist burned with heat I hadn't been expecting. He was hot to the touch, but I resolved that wouldn't stop me. Over and over, my fist found its mark. I thanked Dub for the temporary use of my sight, so my assaults landed true.

The Nain went from playful to angry after the sixth wallop. His hand reached out and coiled around my neck, burning me so badly, I could smell the stench of my own roasting flesh. Every breath I took seared my lungs, filling me with ash and an acrid vengeance I couldn't put a cap on. I wanted to think clearly, to plan my assaults, but something flipped in that moment. I saw red, and wasn't going to stop until I'd killed it.

My fingernails turned to icy shards as I finally tapped into the chill I wasn't all that used to yet. My fingers reached for his eyes, jabbing the tips into the sockets so hard, I could feel the slick of his eyeballs before he blinked. Though the ice melted before it truly cut his eyes, my fingernails showed no mercy.

He wailed at the injustice, and finally, *finally* it was my turn to laugh.

I flattened my fingers and jabbed him there again, over and over until he was so disoriented, he fell off of me, clutching his face in agony. "I can't see! I can't see! Retched little girl! I don't need to see you to burn you alive!" His pain made him speak aloud, instead of echoing his taunting voice inside of my mind.

It was then that I saw how much he'd been holding back. Flames burst out of his palms, licking the walls. The orange tongues climbed skyward, collecting on the ceiling until they were a billowing mass of heat that ate at the roof.

I scrambled to get out, to warn the others. My legs were so injured, I had a hard time moving at all, but somehow I made it to the living room. "Everyone out! The Nain's cracked! Run!" I turned and snatched up Nolan's legs, dragging him as quickly as I could through the living room, and to the front door.

My heart sank when I realized I'd forgotten one very

important thing. My head whipped around, unable to locate much of anything in the sheer chaos. "Lugh, Molly's still in your bedroom!"

Lugh gave up his fight with his Sluagh and bolted toward the Nain Rouge, catching a blast of fire to his arms. His forearms darted up to shield his photo-ready face just in time. His jacket was on fire now, and I knew he'd never make it to Molly at this rate. I bolted down the hall and body-checked my way into Lugh's bedroom, accidentally letting the fire inside.

In the middle of the chaos, there lay the sleeping psycho, hair fanned out around her, and her dress bunched up around her knees.

My shoulder was bloody, but I didn't hesitate. I hoisted Molly up over my injured shoulder and hobbled toward the bedroom door.

When I reached the hallway, I was expecting another fight I might not escape when I heard the Nain Rouge calling for me.

I was not expecting Remy, nor the other headless horsemen who barreled into the house on foot without regard for their own safety.

23

FIRE AND ICE

Molly was lifted from my grip by Remy and taken outside, where the others had been directed. I limped toward the front door in the living room, but Cailleach grabbed my arm. "We have to finish him now!" she shouted over the roar of the fire. The flames were consuming the house, causing the ceiling's beams to start groaning before they began to fall. "We won't get this chance again. Stay with me, and be ready."

"I don't know how to suck things into my ring, Callie! It's just a piece of jewelry to me." Such a fuss that had been made over one single trinket, and I felt utterly unworthy to wield such a powerful tool. I summoned my inner Andre Roussimoff, recalling all the injuries he'd sustained, and still had to play through during his wrestling matches. My giant was fearless, getting the job done no matter what. He was a beacon of strength, and I resolved not to make him ashamed of my efforts in these grave hours.

Cailleach shot an icy blast from her cane as the Nain charged us from the back of the house with his stubby legs. Ice met fire, and it was anyone's guess who might come out on top. The house groaned, and a beam fell from the ceiling between me and my attacker, warning me to venture no further. I held up my hands and gritted my teeth, willing cold to well up inside of me. The stab of ice pricked my palms, shooting out of me at the Nain.

I quickly learned that I had a wallop of an icy punch, but I couldn't sustain it. My help was erratic, and I quickly learned, not enough to save the day. I'm not sure what I'd been expecting; I was a rookie as far as magical ice was concerned.

When a scream erupted from Cailleach as the fire started gaining ground, singeing her fingers, I wasn't sure what to do. Without her to do the heavy lifting, I was a goner. I fished around behind me for anything I could use as a weapon, wishing errantly for a good old-fashioned fire extinguisher. The living room was filled with headless horsemen, who replaced my team's valiant efforts with unwinded, focused blows of their own.

One by one, I watched the Sluaghs drop like flies. The Dullahan fought dirty, and without regard for their own safety. They threw themselves at their prey, stabbing without hesitation over and over again until each Sluagh was properly taught not to mess with the Dullahan.

There was nothing for me to grab to defend myself with, other than the few glass shards on the floor, so I snatched those up. Though, I hoped it wouldn't devolve into hand-to-hand combat again. I merely stood behind Cailleach, ready with my ring, for however she needed to use it.

Her cane was outstretched, and ice tentacles sprang from the handle. Like glass ropes, the ice tried to lasso the Nain, but as soon as they got close, they melted into useless drops. It was difficult to breathe anymore, the smoke taking up residence where there had once been clean air. I watched with hopelessness as Cailleach maintained her distance, as if she was afraid to get her hands dirty. She was staving him off for now, but it was clear that action needed to be taken, or the Nain would soon overpower her. Of the two elements, fire seemed superior to ice.

I heard Bastien's voice shouting from the entrance, warning me to run to him.

I think we both knew I wasn't going to back away now. Not when we'd come this far. Not after the Nain had killed Nolan and attacked my family. No, this was ending today; I wouldn't keep myself up at night, worrying that there was yet more danger targeting me because of my ring. I'd been entrusted to watch over the higher magic, so guard it I would.

Clutching the three shards of glass between my fingers, my faulty legs sprang into action. I didn't wait for Cailleach to exhaust herself trying to best the little red devil. I caught the Nain off-guard when I launched myself at him, my hand clutching the long glass shards between my fingers, so I could fight him Wolverine-style. Hugh Jackman would've been proud.

The Nain had sent his minions after Bastien, the fire filling the edges of the living room. There was no holding me back anymore. I wouldn't be the useless girl whose greatest talent was owning fancy jewelry. I knew who I was, and it wasn't that girl. I ignored Cailleach as I ran through the flames, not stopping for the discomfort of the fire that licked at my clothing. My fist socked the Nain between the eyes, the glass catching on his squishy eyeball. I felt the shards slice between my fingers, but I welcomed the pain; it reminded me I was a fighter, not a waif who scared easily. The Nain had messed with the wrong family, and I wasn't about to let that go unchecked.

"Ah! You blinded me!" the Nain screeched.

I could practically feel Dub patting me on the shoulder, saying, "That's my girl."

I tried my best to summon up Cailleach's blessing she'd given me, shooting the Nain with my blast of ice from my palms at point-blank range. I smiled when his scream froze, and the drops of blood that were cascading down his face turned to crimson dots of ice.

Cailleach shouted out an incantation the likes of which I couldn't follow along with. Then a bright light shot through the cabin. I screamed when Kerdik's ring started heating up. I watched as the Nain Rouge made his last attempts to escape as his thermal body heat rapidly melted my attempt at icing him. He blasted fire in random directions in hopes he would hit us. He was struggling against whatever magicked gravitational pull Cailleach had finally roped him in.

I could smell nothing but burning wood and ash when the Nain dug his heels in, resisting the pull towards my ring, but it was too late for him. In the next breath, he was sucked into the ring, zapping me with an electric shock that rattled my teeth. I tensed muscles I didn't even know I had, my scream trapped in my throat.

When the shock finally released me, my body went limp, crashing to the floor as the house burned and crackled around me. The Nain's evil was gone, but the remnants of his chaos lived on, inching closer to my battle-torn form. I prayed Cailleach wouldn't leave me in here, but as unconsciousness claimed me, I knew those last smoky breaths might be my last.

My eyelids flittered open, catching sight of a headless horseman who wasn't Remy, lifting me from the floor. "I'll get you out of here!" he promised.

I couldn't see where his head was slung, but his voice was a comforting balm that brought about a sense of déjà vu I couldn't quite nail down. It didn't matter, though. By the time my lashes fluttered shut again, the world left me – or perhaps I left the world this time in protest of all the things that threatened to take me out.

24

MAD'S HOME SWEET HOME

"This place is a hole," I heard Cailleach say. "Ye should've told me to port ye anywhere else."

"Word's spread tha the Avalon Rose is a Vampire, so there aren't many places safe for her to travel in Éireland. Can't exactly check ourselves into an inn." Madigan seemed miffed he had to explain his choices to the immortal. "Besides, this is just a place to crash between jobs. Ye want I should hang a wreath on the door?"

Cailleach sighed. "Ye don't even have a proper bed."

"I don't sleep. What would I need a bed for?"

"I'm sure the lasses ye take back here would like a romp on something other than this nest of old blankets ye managed to scrounge up for the Avalon Rose, here."

"The only lass who's ever set foot in this place before today is my Annabelle. She's a good daughter, who doesn't complain about not having things we don't need."

"But you're an Untouchable! Ye know ye could take anything ye want from any vendor, and it's yours. Why ye choose to live like this, I'll never understand."

"The fact tha you'll never understand what it is to be Untouchable doesn't surprise me one bit."

"He's afraid..." I started, but then cut my sentence short with a round of coughing that was deep, and shook my whole body. My head collapsed back into the blankets, keeping me facedown as I hacked my brains out.

"Daisy!" Bastien exclaimed with relief. His hands were on me in the next breath, carefully turning me over and angling me up so Remy could press a glass of water to my lips. I'd been resting on a mess of blankets on the floor of a... a warehouse?

Being able to see was a blessing I didn't take for granted. It had been so long since I'd seen my husband. That Dub hadn't taken my vision away yet made me frantic to drink in the world in a single ocular gulp. I wanted to take it all in and somehow make it a part of me, but I couldn't tear my eyes from Bastien's face. "You." I exhaled out the breath I'd been holding inside for far too long.

His face was lined with worry that hadn't been there the last time I'd seen him. His cheeks looked a little thinner, though not gaunt. It was the small changes that slowly evolved over the course of a year of a person's life, but when you hadn't seen them in a long time, each altered nuance hit you like a freight train. The notch in his left eyebrow was still there – I don't know why this gave me a sense of comfort, but it did. He hadn't shaved in who knows how long, his stubble giving up the fight and mutating into a short beard. It was a sign that he wasn't taking enough time for himself. This past year had been about me – my blindness, my family, my ring, my throne, my fights. Yet Bastien had never complained. He'd put himself on the back burner to take care of me when I'd desperately needed someone to be my rock.

My fingers were shaking when they traced his face, soaking in every detail of the man I loved. "You gave up your cabin in the woods for me." I grimaced at the words that weren't enough. I should've just told him how much I'd missed his face.

Bastien's eyes hardened for a moment, but then turned gentle. "All I had was a cabin in the woods before you, and I'm never going back to that. I don't want it. I want us."

My eyes clouded over with unshed tears, distorting the view of perfection with a hazy crimson. "Of course, the one time I can see you, I can't stop crying."

Bastien froze, his voice lifting with elation. "You can see me?"

I nodded, using one of the edges of the blankets I'd been laid out on to dab at my face. "Is it possible you're even better looking than I've been imagining all this time?"

Now it was Bastien's turn to fight back the tears. To not be able to see was one thing, but to go for so long unable to be seen by the one person you want to know you best? It was a cruelty I wished had never been inflicted on the man I love.

Bastien glanced over his shoulder. "Where can we go for some privacy, Mad?"

"Jays, I knew ye wouldn't last five minutes after she woke. You're addicted, I hope ye know."

"I don't care."

"Tha room over there's mine. There's no bed, though."

"Rosie, you're too injured for that. You'll have to wait until your burns and cuts are a little more healed."

"Oh, Remy says we should wait. Apparently, I'm too injured for your acrobatics."

Bastien kissed my lips, but I didn't let my lashes flutter shut. I was too afraid to close them at all, fearing each glance might be my last. I was mesmerized by his face, needing more. I touched his cheekbones, his hairline, and the crest of his lower lip. It was when I ran my finger along the edge of his eyelashes that I saw a little color rise in his cheeks. He was practically squirming under my intense scrutiny, and loving every second of the undivided attention. So much of me had been divided this past year. "I'm sorry," I whispered.

"There's nothing to be sorry for. You helped capture the Nain Rouge. He's gone, Daisy. Completely gone."

"I'm sorry I couldn't see you." That statement encompassed a myriad of things, and I hoped he would forgive me for each of them. "I see you now."

Bastien ignored our audience and kissed my lips,

tasting like s'mores, cinnamon and man. It was the man part that did me in, making me want more – always more. He was gentle with me, holding back when we both wanted to attack with the full force of our passion.

My eyes flitted to a bandage on his forearm. "Oh, what happened to you? Are you alright?"

A wry smile took over his handsome features. "I'm better off than you are. Just a little slice from a Sluagh. I have new respect for you, offing one of them on your own back in the palace."

"Well, I had Link and Montel there." My heart sank heavy in my breast. Montel had died protecting me, just like Nolan. "The body. Did you get Nolan back to Malone?"

"We did. He's taking the body to his family now. They're going to bury him, and then he said he wants to come back."

I frowned. "What? No way. He should be with his family. His brother just died because he was protecting me. I don't want his family to lose another son. They should be together." Pain pinged my soul. "Oh, Malone lost his twin brother!"

"It's a done deal. Believe me, I tried the same speech on him, but nothing took. Malone's a good soldier. Said he'll leave us once you go back to Common, but not before then. Wants to serve Éireland by helping you cure the Werewolves."

A deep sadness welled in my spirit. I felt myself stretching and growing inside as I digested the scope of such nobility in a person. I hoped that I would be just as altruistic when my limits were tested. I couldn't imagine what it would be like to lose a twin brother. I guessed it would be somewhat more painful than losing Judah or Draper, and I couldn't fathom living through that depth of agony.

My heart ached for Draper, wishing I could see his easy smile, and believe wholeheartedly that it would all be downhill from here. My big brother had a certain way about him that made it seem like the world would figure out a way to be okay, and that I didn't have to be the one to puzzle it all out. I needed someone like that.

Bastien's hand ghosted over my arm, and I winced. "Oh, that smarts. What happened?" I looked down and gasped at the bandages that littered my body. "Whoa, Remy, you really went crazy with the Band-aids."

Remy scolded me as if I was his child. *"Well, you had severe burns all over you, so it was either treat them all, or risk you healing improperly and getting an infection."*

"Sorry. You're the king of all the healing things." I glanced around, finally taking in the company that had picked points around the long, echoing warehouse to focus on, so Bastien and I could have our moment. There were several headless horsemen off in the corner, but one stood closer than the others, as if holding himself back from joining the group of Mad, Remy, Lugh, Bastien, Cailleach and me. "This place – Mad, it's huge. I always pictured you in a tent somewhere, covered in camo and eating bugs and stuff that you hunted off the land."

"Ye want me to eat bugs?"

"This is your house?"

"Aye." His eyes flicked to me, conveying secrets only a few knew. "It's where I lived when I was a lad."

My eyebrows scrunched before revelation hit me. "This is the compound?"

"What's left of it. Link and I burned the rest to the ground, but this part could withstand a decent attack, so we kept it."

Sadness engulfed me. "Mad, why? Why live somewhere that haunts you? Honey, you and Annabelle can come stay with us in Common. Not here."

Madigan was firm. "No. They took too much from me, so I took this from them. It's mine now. Taking whatever land I want is my right as an Untouchable. This is the piece of Éireland I want for myself."

I glanced around at the basically empty airplane hangar. There was a small kitchen nook in the far corner, but it only had the bare basics. "Where's Annabelle's bedroom?"

He pointed to the wall that had nothing near it. "Tha's a false wall. Her room's behind tha."

My gaze flicked back to Madigan, a softness coming over me at the ins and outs that made him who he was. "Of course it is. You love her."

He said nothing to this, but I knew it was true. "She's

with Link and Quinn now, but they'll be bringing her home soon enough. Can ye move? Can ye walk yet?"

"Why wouldn't I be able to walk?"

"You sustained quite a few burns on your legs and arms. Not to mention the scrapes and bruises I found all over you. We're taking it easy today."

"Remy says I'm fine, and we should get going. Heal us up some Werewolves."

Remy threw his hands in the air, exasperated with me. He waved his arms in a very clear "this woman be crazy" gesture at Bastien, who glowered at my attempt to pull the wool over his eyes. "Nice try. We're all in need of a little regrouping. You can't go out as easily anymore. People know you're a Vampire, and that doesn't go over all that well in Éireland."

"They can't hurt me though, right? I mean, I'm wearing your mark."

Bastien's lips tightened. "You were, but it got burned in the fight. You've got to heal up, and then get re-inked. There's no way to tell you're Untouchable like this. The mark's only half there now."

My hand flew to my neck, testing the bandage there. "I probably don't need this."

"You most certainly do need it. Even if there was no political upset, you would still need to lie down. You're badly burned, Rosie. I gave you quite a bit of painkillers so that you could sit up without screaming. Once that wears off, you might have some problems."

Cailleach tapped her cane on the concrete floor. "I should be off. Thanks for helping me capture the Nain Rouge, my child. Ye went above and beyond to finish him. I admit, I didn't know ye would throw yourself at him toward the end."

I tried to tighten my hands into fists, but the bandages stopped me. "He had it coming. It's done though? The Nain's locked up for good now?"

Cailleach nodded once. "He won't be bothering Faîte ever again, thanks to ye fighting when ye could've run."

"What about the Sluaghs?"

"When the Nain was sucked into the ring, they were caught up in it, too." She tapped her cane, seeming to test for something she couldn't detect. "Ye haven't heard from Kerdik yet?"

"He hasn't been by? That's weird. I called him before the fight." I chewed on my lower lip. "Maybe he's making good on his word when he said he was going to stay away this time."

Bastien perked up at this new information.

"Either way, ye still have me," Cailleach reassured us. "I'll be going to help Kerdik and Brìghde track down Dother. Should ye need help with the Werewolves, call me."

I gave her a two-fingered salute. "Roger, Dodger."

Cailleach quirked her blue eyebrow at me, and then vanished to the sound of Christmas bells and a loud *pop*.

"We're without Kerdik, then?" Bastien confirmed. "Any reason?"

"Why hasn't he answered your call, Prim?" Lugh asked. He was sitting upright against the nearest wall – part of the group, yet somehow still separate. I wondered if that's how I would be after living so long with a lifespan that was entirely other – if I would be there but not.

"Said it was too painful. It's not his time yet, and he doesn't want to get in the way." I didn't feel like expounding on that, but let the words settle in the air.

Bastien's hand found my back, rubbing in concentric circles. "That's pretty decent of him not to tear you in two like that."

I swallowed the lump in my throat, not loving that my personal business had managed to make its way out into the daylight. "Everyone else made it out okay? Remy, are these your pals?"

Remy gestured to the headless horsemen who were standing shouting distance away in the long building. *"It takes far more than a few cinders to kill a Dullahan. We're all accounted for. Perhaps you'd like to meet the Phare Dullahan of Éireland. Well, mostly from Éireland. They didn't hesitate to come when I said the Avalon Rose was in trouble. Some of them are anxious to meet you."*

"Well, why are they all the way over there? They're probably afraid I'll bite them or something."

"I assume they're not ignorant of the difference between a Farouche Vamp and an Attelage Vampire. You'll need to

explain it all when you're ready to get up. Lugh kept them away so you could rest. He was worried you might be frightened if you woke up with your sight, and the first thing you saw were my kind."

I offered up a meek smile for Remy. "I like you, and your kind."

"I never assumed anything different. Still, Lugh was clear they stay over there until you awoke."

I glanced over my shoulder to Lugh, who was gazing ahead at nothing in particular, a composed, contemplative look on his face. "Eh, Justin Bieber, you alright over there?"

Lugh turned his chin to lock his eyes on mine. He didn't say anything at first, and I knew he wanted to say that he didn't belong here. I understood the sentiment with everything in me. I didn't belong in Faîte either. "Your adoring fans are waiting to meet ye, Prim," Lugh said without an ounce of a dig in his tone. In his own way, he was one of the few people who got how strange the fame game was. It was nice to know he had my back through it all.

I reminded myself that I was supposed to be some big deal, some royal bigshot whose name alone could rally people she'd never even met. "Could you help me up, Bastien?"

"Sure, Daisy. Easy, now." Bastien and Remy each took a hand and slowly lifted me to my feet. Every part of me was sore.

"Ow! Oh, Remy, something's wrong. My... everything hurts."

I was leaning heavily on Bastien, giving Remy the chance to re-catalog my injuries one by one. There were pink burns with blackened edges on my calves. My knees were scraped, still painted with dried blood that was trying to earn its way to a good scab. My forearms stung too badly to look at when Remy removed the bandages to check them. My neck felt like it was undergoing a perpetual deep cat-scratch. My balance was slightly off from the boom that had rattled my hearing, and my right hand was bandaged so that I couldn't move my fingers. There was precious little that didn't hurt, but I took it in stride. A victory was a victory, no matter how battered we got in the battle.

"Everything's as it should be, my queen. It's going to hurt for a while."

"How about you? Are you and your guys okay?"

I could hear the smile in his voice, and sure enough, when my eyes darted down to the satchel at his side that held his head, his lips were curved up at the edges. *"Your knight is well and accounted for. We didn't lose a single man from our battalion. They came because I told them the Avalon Rose was in trouble. They didn't need the details; they're good men and women who are ready to serve the throne."*

It was a slow effort, but I managed to sink into Remy's embrace, exhaling at the help I'd needed, but hadn't thought to ask for. "Thank you. I don't know what I would've done. One of your guys got me out of the burning house. I don't know who, but I was a goner without him coming in to rescue me."

Remy's hand found my shoulder, and he turned me toward the soldiers in the corner. *"He was overjoyed to be the one to rescue you. Come. Let me introduce you to your army."*

My eyes widened. "Whoa. That sounded way too official. Too 'The Queen's Army'."

"I'll work on the name."

"Let's get this over with, babe." Bastien seemed wary, like he was gearing himself up for something that would be difficult for him. He supported my elbow with one hand, and kept the other at the small of my back – the real estate on my body I knew he was territorial about. I wondered what had Bastien on edge, now that the Nain Rouge was over and done with.

My walk to them was slow, but they didn't rush me. Instead, they made a row and stood at attention – some more polished than others – and waited for me to make my way to them. I was overwhelmed with emotion, imagining what these men and women had been through in their first lives. To have their second lives be so bogged down with Faîte's drama felt unfair. I wanted them to be able to enjoy their new lease on life. Instead they were running into burning buildings and fighting age-old demons – hoping we would win, but not knowing.

"You all don't even know me," I said, flabbergasted at their sacrifice. "But I want to know you. I want to know people who would give up their shot at having a second chance to be free and do what they wanted, just to help us clean up a mess you didn't make. I want to know all of you so that I can be more like you. You didn't care about your own safety; you cared about everyone in Faîte." I pressed my hand over my heart, moved at the heroes who stood before me. "Thank you for rescuing us."

There was a man who was first in line and seemed to speak for the group. His head was slung under his arm in a leather sling, his eyes connecting with mine as he spoke from his body's hip. It was totally trippy. "Aye, Queen Rosie. Our swords are yours, if you'll have us."

I nodded but felt the need to put all the cards on the table first. "I'll take all the help I can get, but there are a few things you should know first." I ignored Bastien's grip on my elbow that told me to take the servitude and run with it. If they were going to sign their lives away, they deserved to know who they were following. "Remy told you we're going to round up the Werewolves, right?"

"Aye, my Queen. We're ready to honor our kinsmen by helping with tha."

"I need them brought in alive, if that's possible. The Werewolves don't know what they're doing when they transition. I don't want to kill innocent people."

"Aye. Tha's one of the reasons we're all here. We've been stopping vigilante Were hunts whenever we can. Remy said there was a queen who could put an end to their suffering without slaughtering them, so tha's why we're here."

I nodded, chewing on my lower lip before I spoke again, sifting out the right words, if there were any. "You should know who you're following. It's not fair otherwise. I'm an *Attelage* Vampire."

Bastien moved his shoulder to partially stand in front of me, using himself as my shield. Madigan trotted up from behind and closed in on the other side, creating a wall between myself and the Dullahan. Even from social scorn, they would protect me. My heart swelled with love for the Untouchables.

I touched both men on the smalls of their backs and slowly parted their bodies, so I could address the men and women. "King Urien doesn't think my kind should be allowed to live among the people. He thinks *Attelage* Vamps are dangerous. The only person I'm a danger to is Bastien, and he's decided he's okay with me being this way. I won't bite any of you, and if I feed regularly, I'm a totally normal person. It really doesn't affect anyone, except Bastien. I just thought you should have all the information, so you don't feel shanghaied later on. If you want out, I totally understand."

Bastien reached behind him and gripped my good hand, letting me know that he didn't agree with my decision to open myself up to ostracism, but he understood it. He understood *me*, and that was no small mercy.

I held my breath as my gaze flicked to the frowns on the faces that hung in various places on the soldiers' bodies. I wasn't sure what to make of some of the expressions. Some avoided my gaze as if I might be contagious. There were a few people who looked nonplussed at the information, and a couple others who wore their heads on their backs, keeping their reactions as a total wild card I couldn't predict, but for the nervous shifting of feet.

One man took a step back, raising his hands as if in defeat. "I'm sorry, lass, but I can't serve a Vampire. I lost my mammy to a bloodsucker, so to follow ye would be to turn my back on her. I can't."

25

ROMEO AND JULIET

 nodded, keeping my face composed. I kept Lane in my heart, remembering who I was. "I completely understand. I hope you have a great life, man. And thank you for saving us. If it's any consolation to your conscience, you fought to save the Untouchables, and assisted an immortal. When you tell the story to your friends, you can leave me out of it, so you don't have to feel torn. I wouldn't want you to sully your mother's memory like that. Makes total sense."

His eyes closed, pained at my acceptance, as if that had been worse than me banishing him or something. "You're a true queen, if ever I saw one. Gracious to your very last breath. Thank ye, your majesty." He had the humility and kindness to bow to me before making his exit out the back door (or the front door. The whole thing was basically a warehouse with no clue as to which end one would lay the welcome mat. Come to think of it, this was Mad's place, so the chances there was a welcome mat to speak of were pretty slim).

Lugh spooked me when he spoke over my shoulder. "Anyone else care to look down on the Avalon Rose because she was infected with a disease she won't harm anyone with? Anyone want to tell Cross Shot when he's armed with his bow tha she's not worthy of knights like yourselves?" His hand touched my hip as he stepped forward, posturing to tell me he literally and figuratively had my back.

I laced my fingers through his and squeezed in appreciation. "It's alright, Lugh. If they're going to stay, they should be here without the threat of Cross Shot." I put my hands on Mad and Bastien, parting them further so I could step forward and see more fully. "Or the Untouchables."

Madigan snarled down at me. "I'll not see my wife talked down to, like she's not worthy of an army."

It never stopped catching me off-guard when Link or Madigan referred to me as their wife. I leaned up on my toes and pecked his prickly cheek. "Thank you, but I want a loyal army, not one that's afraid."

"Aye. Tha, I'll accept. Best weed out the weak now." He turned with a scowl to the others, and I knew if I didn't intervene, he would take it upon himself to train them, and make their lives miserable.

"I've got this, sweetie." I stepped forward to address

them. "So can I assume you're all cool with me being who I am?"

They answered with varying degrees of certainty, but it was enough to convince me I wasn't going to get a Columbian necktie in my sleep. The main dude in charge brought his head forward to more clearly display his face. "I'm Patrick, your majesty, at your service. We're ready to round up the Werewolves at your command. We all have weapons enough to make our enemies useless."

I moved toward him and shook his hand. It was counter-intuitive to address his midsection, where his head hung. It was laterally off, and I had a hard time not glancing up at his shoulders to address the empty space there. I was determined to learn, though. "It's nice to meet you, Patrick. I'm Rosie."

I moved to the next person, who was a woman. "Your majesty, I'm Kellyn. I died four decades ago, so I'm not apprised of everything tha's been happening in Faîte. All I know is tha Remy said ye don't have a problem with us not having heads, and tha ye would find a use for us. I have no family anymore, so the Phare Dullahan are my people now. If Remy says ye are worth following, tha's the direction I'll set my stride."

I glanced over to Remy, who was standing on Bastien's other side. He stood with his hands behind his back, but his eyes were trained on Kellyn, sneaking glances I could tell he wasn't used to being tempted by. "Of course I don't have a problem with you having a head or not. You are who you are. Just no riding on horses, okay? That whole 'someone dies every time a Dullahan stops riding' thing isn't something I want happening on my watch. That cool?"

"Of course. Remy said ye were of good quality. I don't care if you're a Vampire if you've already mated. I just want to belong again."

I heard the loneliness in her voice and knew that intense sting of ostracism. Before I could rein myself in, I flung my arms around her shoulders, in hopes I might be able to squeeze the lonesomeness out of her. "You can belong with us. That's basically our entire group – a bunch of people who don't belong anywhere."

I'm not going to lie, it was weird when her severed head started crying on her hip. Her arms gripped me, clinging to my shirt as if she was afraid to be released in the boys' club where, again, she didn't belong. Her need for a simple hug was palpable, and I was grateful that, of all my shortcomings, I could provide her with this most basic of needs. "Thanks, Queen Rose."

"Just Rosie, Kellyn. We'll get through this, alright?" Queen of Avalon didn't quite suit me anymore. I felt more pride in being Queen of the Misfits, which, given who I was, felt like the perfect place for me.

I released her with a smooch to her shoulder, since bending over and kissing her cheek seemed awkward. Then I moved on down the line, shaking hands, thanking them, trying to match the faces with the names, and then both those things with the body. I had a feeling I'd be calling most of them "dude" just to be safe.

Bastien was at my side for each introduction, until we reached the man on the end, at which point, he took a step back. Dude's head was slung on his back, so I addressed where his head would've been, were it still attached to his shoulders. He had a familiar scent to him that hit me again with that wave of déjà vu. "You... You're the dude who rescued me in the fire. You ran back into the burning building to pull me out."

"Yes, your majesty."

There was something about his voice that dinged a bell inside of me. His majestic and poised frame didn't tower over me but kept his shoulders just five inches above mine. His accent wasn't Éirish, but Avalonian. "You're from Avalon, right? What are you doing in Éireland, soldier?"

"I heard the Avalon Rose was in Éireland, so I made my way over here as soon as I could. I tracked down Remy, who I knew would have an idea of how to find you."

I gaped at him. "Seriously? Wow. Thank you. You couldn't have better timing. What's your name, soldier?"

There was a cheeky smile in his reply. "Well, now that cuts me to the quick. Has it truly been that long, Princess?"

There was something both reverent and teasing about the way he said "princess." I couldn't put my finger on it, but I knew this guy. "Who are you? Do we know each other?"

I heard his chuckle and could practically match the

small crinkles on the outside of eyes I knew. Somehow I could picture indulgent green eyes, even though he still hadn't let me see his face. "You asked me to marry you, once upon a very long time ago. Would that I could've saved you from that awful day where you were auctioned off. Though it seems you're in good hands now. Bastien the Bold is quite the choice to settle down with. I'd hoped you would marry well, and that, you did."

"I asked you to marry me?" I flipped through the short list of people I'd popped that particular question to. "I'm not sure it's me you're thinking of, pal. The only guy I asked that of, aside from Bastien, died a long time ago."

"Ah. How very tragic. Was he a good man?"

I choked on a lump in my throat. "He was wonderful, but I don't like to talk about him. I loved him very much, and it got him killed." I didn't like saying all of this, least of all in front of Bastien. I shot him an apologetic glance over my shoulder, for which he offered up a weak smile. I frowned when I turned back to the headless dude who seemed to only speak in riddles. "Did you know him?"

"Who? I know a lot of people."

I shook my head, not wanting to say Demi's name aloud. It was too sad, and he'd been precious to me at a time in my life where I'd been cast aside by too many people. Demi had looked at me as if I was something special, and after a while it started to remind me that I was. "Never mind. Thank you for pulling me out of the building, and for coming to rescue all of us."

"Of course. Romeo would never abandon Juliet to the fire."

I froze, uncertain if I'd heard him wrong, or if my ears were just latching onto what they wanted to hear. "I... Where did you hear about Romeo and Juliet? That story's from Common."

"Indeed. A beautiful princess told me the tale. It was all that got me through the night I was beaten to teach her a lesson. Though, I see you're still wearing jeans, so I don't think Morgan's teaching methods were all that effective."

I gasped, scandalized. "How dare you talk about Demi like that! I don't know how you found out about that conversation between him and I, but it was private. In fact, my whole life with him is private, believe it or not. Demi's not a joke. I won't let you take what was precious to me and talk about him like it was all no big deal." I whirled, facing Madigan as I jerked my thumb over my shoulder. "This clown's out. I won't stand for an ounce of anyone joking about Demi getting beaten because he was close to me."

"Juliet, you misunderstand me."

Bastien didn't look nearly as indignant as I thought he should, but instead looked away, as if bracing himself for the inevitable. "You two have a lot to talk about. No one comes near Mad's place, so why don't you two go on a walk and figure all of this out."

I balked at Bastien, confused as to why he was looking

beaten down, instead of his usual brash self by my side. "Bastien?"

"It's fine, Daisy. Go catch up. Just stay on the property."

I turned toward the Dullahan who'd caused me so much heartache with a few sentences. He flipped his sack around, so that his head was facing me, giving me a blast of something that nearly bowled me over. I swear my brain skipped a beat when the dark lashes blinked up at me and the sculpted lips I'd kissed too many times to count whispered my name like a prayer.

26

BACK WHEN WE WERE US

ainting wasn't something I'd done a whole lot of in my life before coming to Faîte, least of all from shock. When my eyes opened, my heart nearly leapt out of my chest at the fact that I could still see. When I confirmed one of the people hovering over me was Demi, my heart seemed on the verge of giving out. "You... I... It's not possible! Bastien, he's not real! There's some funky magic crap happening, because you're dead!"

Bastien and Remy helped me to sit up, while Remy pressed a cup of water to my trembling lips. *"All of us are supposed to be dead,"* Remy reminded me. *"Demi was decapitated, remember?"*

"I held your head in my hands! When Morgan had me thrown down into the well, they cut off your head and tossed it down there to torture me! You were the only person with me in the dark, but you were dead!

They killed you!" Though I knew it was supposed to make sense, since he fit the profile of a Dullahan, my brain still rejected the notion. "Your head was decomposing, but it looks brand new in your sling there. It's not possible!"

Patrick fielded my nervous breakdown. "None of this is possible. This is part of the higher magic tha escaped back into the world when everything spilled out of your ring. It reanimates the decapitated. We were all in various states of decay. Kellyn's been dead for decades, but she stands before ye looking sharper than ever." At this, Kellyn postured. "Tha makes sense why ye went back into the burning cabin, Demi. We all assumed Cailleach had ye, your majesty, but Demi didn't trust your safety, so he ran back inside to drag ye out."

I was on the verge of bursting into tears. I could feel the pressure building behind my eyes and didn't want to do this in front of everyone. "Walk with me?" I asked, confused and mesmerized by the headless man kneeling before me.

"Of course."

Bastien and Remy helped me to my feet, which felt like the unsteady legs of a newborn deer at the moment. Bastien squeezed my hand, bringing my focus back to him. "Come back to me after you catch up, okay?"

My heart ached with guilt that we had the kind of relationship where he had to worry about things like that. "Always. This doesn't change us."

Bastien drew in a full breath, as if he'd needed that confirmation. "Go ahead, then. I trust you."

Lugh frowned at Demi. "I don't know this bloke. Is she safe wandering around outside with him?"

Bastien sucked in his lower lip before answering. "Demi was Rosie's *soumettre* back when she was living with Morgan le Fae a couple years ago."

Lugh's eyebrows shot skyward. "Ye took yourself a *soumettre,* did ye? Well, well. I didn't know ye had tha in ye, Prim."

I pinched the bridge of my nose. "It wasn't like that. I... Oh, never mind."

Lugh wrapped his leather jacket around my shoulders, giving me a little squeeze. "It's cold outside."

"Thanks. I'll be careful." It was with painstaking slowness that I walked with Demi out into the cold. The icy air hit me like a slap across the face. Intrusive and aggressive was the chill that made the jacket's efforts seem laughable. The snow was up to my knees, but still we waded through so we could get a little privacy to catch up.

I saved all my words for when we were a safe distance from the door of the bunker, and then everything spilled out of me in a rush. "Morgan told me Avril had you killed because she wanted to hurt me. She wanted the ring Kerdik gave me, so she took you from the castle to punish me for not giving her the ring. At the time, I dug my heels in because I didn't want to be manipulated, but I made the wrong choice! I didn't know she would kill you. I had no idea that was even a possibility. Please, Demi. You have to know that I would have traded anything to get you back. You were... I had no one. Just utterly no one, but you were there for me, and I abandoned you to Avril!" My voice picked up with emotion, and I knew there was no point in holding back the tears now. The winter wonderland blurred red as the blood fell from my tear ducts. I didn't want to stain Lugh's coat, so I scooped up a fistful of snow and pressed it to my cheeks, catching the drops as they rolled.

"Rosie, what's happening to your face? Why is there blood?" he fretted, touching my chin as his eyebrows creased with concern.

"Oh, it's nothing. I cry blood now. It's a long story. I guess you could say all the magic in this place got me pretty good."

"Does it hurt?"

I peered into his sharp green eyes, seeing compassion I knew I didn't deserve. "Living without you? Knowing your death was my fault? That was the worst kind of hurt. You should hate me. You clearly don't know it was all because of me."

"Oh, Juliet. That wasn't your fault."

"I'm the reason you didn't get to go back to your family!" Guilt squeezed me around the throat, making my voice come out squeaky and strained. "Then Morgan threw your head down the well into the dark with me, and I was so afraid for you! Even though you were already dead, I talked to you like you were still there. I lost my mind for a while because I didn't want to be without you! I told you every secret I ever had, sang you every song I could think of." I glanced skyward as my tone turned woeful. "They were Lugh's songs, only I didn't know it at the time! I tried everything because I didn't want you to be scared down there. Tell me the weird magic didn't give you access to that period. Tell me you weren't scared in the dark!"

Demi stopped walking and drew his arms around me. "Sweet girl, I don't recall any of that. I was long gone by that point, though I do wish I had access to all your secrets. The things you must've confessed to me down there. Morgan really threw you down into a well? Which one?"

"The one on the back of the property they don't use for fresh water. She had Rigs do it. He didn't want to, but you know the job."

Demi stiffened. "I know the job well enough, but I can't forgive Rigby for such an offense. He knew how I felt about you."

"I don't think any of that mattered. Morgan wanted what she wanted, so Rigs delivered."

"That must've been terrible for you."

"It was terrible for *you*!" I all but shouted at him over the wind. I was freezing, but I was in Demi's arms. I didn't care if my toes fell off at that point; I was in Demi's arms – a place I never thought I'd be again. "I know I'm married, so it's neither here nor there, but I have to know." I choked on the words, and for a moment, I feared the question that burned my insides might be stuck in me forever. "Was it all real, you and me? It's fine either way, I just need to know. Was it fake? Did Morgan order you to seduce me? Were we real? Was any of it?" I closed my eyes, bracing myself against the answer I didn't think I was ready for.

Demi's fingers wound through my tangles in the expert way only he knew how to do. He'd braided my hair, done fancy styles, and even played with the tresses to lull me to sleep. He gave my curls a tug to let me know he was serious. "Morgan assigned me to be your *soumettre*, but that was no secret. In the beginning, she wanted me to ask you certain questions and find out information that might lead her to the missing Jewels of Good Fortune, but I told her you didn't have the answers."

"But you didn't ask me anything about the jewels."

"I know. I didn't want them in Morgan's hands any more than you did. From the beginning, you owned me. You looked at me like I was a person, so I remembered to be one. I started to believe that I had choices, and even though I was a slave, in my heart, you made me feel like a man. You truly didn't know of my devotion to you?"

My cheeks pinked. "Bastien told me you were hired to be my boyfriend, so Morgan could use you to manipulate me."

The muscles in Demi's cheeks stiffened. "I suppose he would say that. I was meant to be Morgan's pawn, yes, but I loved you from the start. When we were apart, I wrote you poetry and drew sketches of your lovely face. I sought out new books to read to you, new games to bring about your smile."

I chewed on my lower lip as I let the bloody snow fall to the ground. I hoped my face was somewhat clean. "Rigby gave me the book of your poems – your journal. I have them at my place in Common."

"Then you should know how true my love for you was."

I burrowed into his chest, clutching his coat in hopes that he wouldn't run away from me at my confession. "I can't read, Demi. I've never been able to read more than a few sentences, and I didn't want anyone else reading your private journal, so I don't know what's in there, other than the sketches."

"Surely you can..." I could practically hear him flipping through all the memories of us curled up in bed with *him* reading to *me*, and not the other way around. "You can't read," he said as the truth dawned on him. "I had no idea."

"Not too many people in Faîte do. I'm not stupid," I promised, hoping that was true, and praying he believed me. "It's just the way my brain works." I watched Demi's features for signs of flight, but they never came. Instead, his cold knuckles brushed down my cheek as they had hundreds of times before, back when we were us.

"Then let me tell you what I confessed to the servants, and to my journal. You were the kindest, gentlest, loveliest woman I'd ever known. That I got to kiss you, tease you, and hold you while you slept on my chest? I would've given anything to marry you, Juliet."

"I would've gone through with it, I think, given more time."

Demi's eyes closed, battling with the life that could've been, and accepting what now was. "Is Bastien a good husband to you?"

"He is. More loyal than I deserve most days. He's a good guy."

"Then that's all that matters. That I get to see you in this second life? Be near you and watch you redeem Faîte? Despite everything, that makes me a very fortunate man."

"See? That you can say that makes you a rare treasure."

His fingers gripped my hair, tugging lightly at the roots. "I think I had my own doubts over whether or not you loved me as I loved you. To hear you call me a treasure? After everything I was forced to do in my previous life, that's a gift I won't soon forget." He moved us closer to the bunker to shield us from the wind. "Avril wasn't new to me. She'd requested me several times before. But that last time, I couldn't do it. I tried to be obedient, but my body belonged only to you by that point, and wouldn't rouse under her touch. She was... quite disappointed."

I knew he was holding back for my sake, so I could only imagine the horrors he'd had to endure at her hands. "Demi, all of it was my fault. Avril wanted Kerdik's ring. I should've given it to her. If I had, none of this would've happened!"

"Ah, you say that like the Daughters of Avalon could be satisfied with just one more trinket, just one more jewel. If you had, it soon would've been another prize she would've stolen me to get at. It's just how they are."

"I'm sorry, Demi. Please don't forgive me. Be mad and punish me for letting you die. I promise you, no matter how angry you get, it's nothing to the guilt I've felt every day since you died."

"You gave me a life before my death. I could never be mad at the woman who gave me that. I could never be cross with you, Juliet."

I melted at the nickname we'd used so long ago. "Always the same Romeo, even in your second life. Man, I fell hard for you."

"I knew it was a fool's hope to think you might still be an unmarried maiden when I found you. As soon as I got my head back, I went to my family, and then went straight to the castle, prepared to ask King Urien for your hand. So much has changed since I died. Some for the better, and some for the worse."

"That seems to be how life goes," I commented, indulging probably too long in the embrace that soothed an ache in me I'd pretended it was normal to live with. His chest was solid, but leaner than Bastien's burly one. Demi had been a light for me during a very dark time. Even years later, I clung to him as such. "Rigby still lives in the palace with me. We moved past the well incident enough for me to trust him in the house."

"I don't want to talk about Rigby. Tell me that if you weren't married, I would be making love to you right here, right now in this very snow. Tell me I'm not a monster to you in this form."

"Of course you're not a monster." I didn't dare answer the other part. "Who told you that?"

"My family couldn't get rid of me quick enough. I knew my position in the palace brought them great shame, but I thought that when I returned a free man, they would be overjoyed. My mother shrieked that her boy was a deformed creature, and my father escorted me off the property – the land he'd been given in exchange for me."

The ice hardened in my veins. "You've got to be joking. Demi, no. Do you even have a place to stay?"

"None of the Dullahan do. That's why we stick together, travel in packs. Together, we're terrifying to the people, so no one messes with us. On our own? Well, it's best we're together. That's why we're always looking for others like us, so they don't have to be alone, either."

"You need land. When we get back, I'll work something out with Lot, so the Dullahan can have their own property. You're so right, though. How would Kellyn have a place to stay? She lost her life forty years ago. Her house would have another family living in it by now. I didn't even think about it. Totally self-involved of me. What else do you need?"

"Nothing but a place to rest my head. I do grow weary of carrying it around." His soft smile seemed to believe the best in me, even when I felt like I was the absolute worst. "Thank you. Once again, you saved me with your graciousness."

I scoffed in dismay. "I never saved you. I couldn't save you. You died, and I was stuck in that stupid well, not even able to save myself."

"You gave me dignity I'd forgotten I was allowed to have. Everyone else stole me, but you were the one woman I wanted to give myself to – the sweet girl who was too shy to ask for what she wanted." His voice grew husky with need. "Tell me you wanted me."

My heart thrummed with a blush that seemed to take over my whole body. My admission came out in a whisper. "You know I did."

My reply seemed to settle some unreconciled part in him, allowing his disquiet to finally rest. "How I loved you, Juliet."

My hand trailed up and rested on his chest. "Oh, Romeo. I loved you, too."

27

THE NEW WIFE

We warmed ourselves by the fire Madigan built from his enormous stockpile of wood. We'd been chilling in the bunker for five days, until I'd been ruled ready to kick butt. Or more likely, stand there while everyone around me kicked butt, and I had to be the girl on the sidelines, making sure I didn't break a nail, lest the whole kingdom collapse. *Lame.*

I wasn't handling my position all that well. The Phare Dullahan had submitted to being trained by Madigan, who was the most unmerciful dictator I knew. I tried to unofficially train with them, but Remy freaked out when he saw the first bruise on my knee when I collapsed from too many pushups. The point was to do them until we collapsed – Mad had said as much. I'd made it past two of the Dullahan, which I was quite proud of. Bastien kept pace with me until Remy overruled me training any further. Then I got to see what my husband could really do. Bastien the Bold wasn't Untouchable for no reason. Despite our life of leisurely country habits in Common, Bastien hadn't missed a beat from his old military days. He outlasted everyone, and then shot me a devilish grin. "I can go a few more rounds. Why don't you sit on my back, Daisy? Give me a real challenge."

"Show off!" I accused, mildly miffed that he beat me by a jillion miles. Despite my defeat, I couldn't help but gawk. Bastien in action was a sight to see. I was so grateful Dub hadn't taken my vision away. I got to witness every bead of sweat that cascaded down Bastien's forehead, and cherished every second of it.

Mad was ready to move onto the next thing on the agenda, but didn't want to cut Bastien short on his epic pushup battle with himself. He pressed his boot to the middle of Bastien's back, adding just enough pressure for Bastien to strain through the effort. The more he grunted through his pushups, I only wanted him more. Ever since my sight and Demi had come back into my life, and I'd made it clear that I was still very much married, Bastien had gotten back a little of his play. He'd been too serious for so long. It was good to see him grin. Heck, it was good to see him at all. We didn't take for granted the fact that I could see him again, but took full advantage of the luxury. Every flirty touch was amped up now, and he didn't hold back when he tickled my side, tugged on my curls, or danced his fingers across my belly whenever he passed by me. He was reveling in being chosen, and I was just glad someone like him wanted someone like me.

Bastien finally gave up his fight to do the most pushups ever in the history of calisthenics when a voice I knew and adored broke through the fascination everyone had with the Bastien show. "Is he really showing off without me? It's not a real competition unless I'm in the mix."

"Link!" I whirled toward the entrance and ran to him, elated that I could get where I wanted without a guide. He held out his arms, and I crashed into him. My arms coiled around his neck so I could kiss his cheek over and over. "You're here! Oh, I missed you. You're exactly what this place needs."

"Ye can see me?" Link asked with excitement dancing in his eyes as he assessed me. At my nod, he let out a giant "whoop" and wrapped his arms around my hips, lifting me off the ground so he could smooch my lips. "Am I handsomer than ye remembered?"

"Not possible. You were the perfect specimen before. Can't improve upon the Best in Show." I noted the crinkles at the corners of his eyes that had always been there, but somehow looked that much more boyish and joyful. "You look happy."

"Tha, I am. I've got my Quinny, and now I've got my wee Rose. I'm a lucky lad, indeed."

"Oh, you charmer."

"I'm *your* charmer," he reminded me with a caddish grin.

"Well, then I guess I'm a lucky lass. I missed you a hundred thousand times, Link. Éireland without you? What's the point?"

"I can't think of a single one. But I have a good reason. A very good reason why it took me so long to come back."

"It better involve all sorts of presents and unicorns that you brought for me."

"Aye, something even better. I brought ye a wife."

My eyebrows scrunched together in confusion. "But I'm already married. To a dude."

"Da!" came the squeaky voice from the doorway behind Link. Annabelle's scarred face was beaming at the sight of her adoptive father. "Da, I'm home!"

Madigan was known for having one facial expression, but for the nine-year-old cutie pie, he birthed a second. The smile was one of relief and adoration. To the untrained eye it might've looked like a grimace, but I knew better.

Annabelle limped toward him, but Madigan ran to her, scooping her up so she didn't have to bother with the arduous task of walking. Man, she had him wrapped around her little finger. It was adorable, and exactly what Mad needed if he ever wanted to morph into a human someday, instead of the cyborg he'd been trained to be. "Home, ye are. This place was empty without ye."

Annabelle's thin arms wrapped so securely around Mad's neck that I could tell he'd stopped breathing, rather than tell her it was too tight a grip. "Da, never send me away again. I don't belong with her!" She spoke the word "her" like she'd been sent off to live with a rattlesnake. My head jerked to where Quinn was standing at the entrance, her hands folded in front, her chin downcast with meekness she couldn't divorce from her personality. I couldn't believe Annabelle hadn't taken a shine to Quinn. Girlfriend was amazing.

Link motioned for Quinn to come stand with him. "Rosie, I brought ye home a wife. Meet my Quinny. Officially *my* Quinny."

I let out a shriek that lifted me up onto my toes. I turned full-on sorority girl, complete with clapping my hands and then covering my mouth through a second scream of elation. "That's the best news in the universe!" I threw my arms around Quinn, hugging her tight as I bobbed up and down on the balls of my feet. I kissed her all over her face until she was laughing and grinning. "Welcome to the family! Oh, I'm so glad for you both!"

"Thanks, Rosie. I'm still a little shocked myself. After I was cast out, I didn't think marriage would happen for me again, least of all to someone like Link."

I jumped continuously, like a bunny who couldn't stop herself. I kissed her cheek, then Link's, and then hers again. "Oh, tell me all about the wedding. Were there flowers? Tell me there were flowers. Tell me there was music and you wore a pretty dress."

Color crept into Quinn's cheeks as the Dullahan gathered around to listen in on the commotion, and gawk at the newest Untouchable to join our group. "It was a little too sudden for any of tha. Link asked me to marry him, and the moment I said yes, he jumped up, swept me off my feet and carried me to the nearest city judge. Our engagement was all of an hour before we were married."

Link shrugged unapologetically. "What? I didn't want her changing her mind on me. Hot commodity like her? I wasn't going to wait around to lock tha down."

I covered my mouth with my hand to stifle the giggle. "I hope you never change an inch, Link. Always be the guy who makes his own rules. Promise me."

He sweetly kissed my nose. "I do."

"Ye aren't blind no more," Quinn observed. "I like the look of ye with a smile. Far better a world this is, now tha's in place."

"We're sisters now! I mean, we always were, but you're in the Brotherhood, which means we're sisters!" I started hopping again when I saw her neck tattoo, too elated for my feet to anchor themselves to the ground. There had been too much harrowing action as of late. I needed something to celebrate.

Quinn laughed and threw her arms around me to squeeze more giggles from my body. "Aye. We always were sisters. How I missed ye, Rosie." She sighed contentedly, no doubt missing the female companionship that sometimes got lost in the boys' club.

I didn't hold back my grin from her as Bastien attacked Link with the sweatiest hug known to man. "You got married without me? Don't tell me you also had your honeymoon without me, too!"

"Of course not. Ye know I've been saving myself for your hairy arse." Link laughed, clapping his friend on the back. The hug didn't end at Bastien's usual three-second mark. I watched with adoration for the two as the wrestling hold that had passed for a hug melted into something sweeter. A rare brush of sincerity painted Link as a wiser man when he whispered, "It's a grand thing to see ye happy, brother."

A whine from the door cut the sweet mood with an ice pick. "Are ye really hugging him, Link? He's all sweaty. Bastien, wash up first. I can smell ye from over here."

I watched Bastien's carefree body language stiffen, and his shoulders tighten with that same tension he exhibited when he was gearing up for a fight. "But how can you smell me with your nose in the air?" Then to Link, he said, "You had to bring Katya? Why?"

Link clapped Bastien twice on the shoulder, telling him to rally. "Nicholai heard ye were going to heal the Werewolves, and he wanted to help."

"How did he hear about tha?" Lugh asked, coming into the fray.

"It's spreading its way around Faîte like wildfire. Cailleach was talking ye up, Rosie. Kerdik spread word, too. It's giving the nations hope tha the lost magic might not destroy the land. Avalon's rounding up their Werewolves now so tha when you're finished here, ye can go heal the rest of Faîte."

I pinched the bridge of my nose. "Oh, man. Okay. We should probably get going on this, then. How soon until the troops are ready to go, Mad?"

"We can set out tonight, but Katya stays here. Where's Nicholai?"

Katya's voice was higher pitched and a little nasally. She remained in the doorway, as if Mad's place was disgusting. I mean, it wasn't exactly a homey cottage on a hill, but Mad didn't tolerate mess or dust, so the bunker was clean, at least. "My husband's watering the horses. I'm staying here for a while, at least until Lamar is healed." Katya looked around the bunker and sniffed as if it had offended her by not being the Ritz. She had blonde hair that went down to her waist, an upturned, slender nose, and a fancy yellow dress that accentuated her pear-shaped figure.

"Your brother needs a healer?" Bastien inquired.

"Lamar needs the Avalon Rose. He was infected with the Werewolf curse, so we brought him here. Such a whiner about the whole thing. I mean, honestly. Mother couldn't wait for ye to work your way to his village, ye understand. But if you're done with your little vacation now, perhaps ye could heal my brother so he could go back to his oh-so-satisfying career as an ironsmith." She rolled her eyes, as if that was a laughable vocation. "Madigan, seriously, if I have to get my things from the coach…" She snapped her fingers at him.

I'd met too many girls like her in my life, but they usually left me alone, unthreatened by my hump and wonky eye. I didn't want to be put off by her attitude, and truly believed that kindness was a powerful healing balm that everyone needed. I worked up my beamiest smile and aimed it at her as I moved around Link and Quinn, and stuck out my hand. "It's nice to meet you, Katya. I'm Rosie."

Her upper lip curled at my offering. "I'm sure ye are. Ye can help Nicholai with the bags, then. You're certainly dressed for manual labor."

"Don't ye be nasty to my Auntie Rose," Annabelle shouted, clearly having hit her limit after traveling with the woman for who knows how long.

I shot Annabelle a wink. "It's alright, babe. I don't mind helping. Just out front?"

"Obviously. And don't let my bags get wet from the snow. I have delicate silks in one of them."

"No problem." I got to the door, but the second I touched the handle, no less than ten male voices rebuked me. "What?"

Demi and Patrick trotted over to the door and opened it. "You don't fetch bags, Juliet," Demi reminded me with a slight scold.

"Um, neither do you. You're not a servant in this life, Demi. That was your old life."

"Well, you're a queen in this life, so that means you

don't touch door handles or carry bags. Patrick and I can get them."

"You don't have to do that. I'm not useless."

"You're confusing 'useless' with 'treasured'. Besides, it's too cold out for you to be running around without a coat. Back in the bunker with you, now."

I shot Demi a faux glower, but it soon died into a humble respect as I ran my fingers over his hair. His head hung in its sling on his hip, and he closed his eyes and smiled at the small offering of contact. "Thanks, guys. You really don't have to do that."

"Our pleasure, Rosie," Patrick said as he opened the door and went out into the snow with Demi.

Annabelle wore a no-holds-barred frown as she clung to her daddy. "No, no. Da, tell Katya she can't stay with us."

Madigan's expression went back to that same old hardness. "Untouchables take care of their own. Nicholai married her, so tha makes her your Aunt Katya."

Annabelle sulked that she'd been overruled. "Alright, but she can't have my bedroom."

"Aye, tha's fine. Are ye well? Ye look thinner than when I saw ye last."

Annabelle pointed a finger in accusation at Katya. "She made pig noises every time I ate a bite!"

"She did what?" Mad's head whipped to Katya, his nostrils flared.

Katya's raised chin didn't feel the need to lower itself. "Do ye really think it's wise for her to gain weight when she's limping how she is? How can tha be good for her leg?"

Quinn held up her hand. "I separated them for a while after that. Annabelle eats with Link and me now. Ye don't need to worry, Madigan, sir."

Link's arm around Quinn reassured her. "Ye don't need to call him 'sir'. Ye never needed to do tha. Mad's just as married to ye as I am now."

Mad gave her a nod and made eye contact for two solid seconds, which had to be some sort of record. That was his official "welcome to the family," or "what he said." I remembered from my own induction.

Bastien bowed to Quinn, and then reached out to take her hand, placing a light kiss on the back as his own welcome. "Good to see you again, hun." Then he shot me a smirk and pulled Quinn in for a tight hug, being gentle as he kissed her pinked cheek. "What a lovely wife you are."

I grinned that he was being sweet to her, and that she was being doted on like the queen she was. Anyone who could rein in Link the way she did with her gentle hand deserved a crown of some sort. I wrapped my arms around her again once Bastien released her, grateful for a friendly face in the sea of too much testosterone. "I'm so very glad you're here." I held Quinn tight, and hoped that being near me wouldn't bring too much trouble her way.

28

THE FEU FOLLET

"I feel like we should be quiet. I mean, we are sneaking, aren't we?"

"Not sneaking. The opposite, in fact. We should be making as much noise as we can." Patrick had a pole over his shoulder that had an animal carcass on it. I tried not to grimace at the panther's lifeless tail flapping in the breeze. "We want to bring the Weres to us, catch them all in one go, if we can."

"I guess. It just feels off." I held onto Demi's waist as his donkey trotted through the snow. Every time a member of the Dullahan rode on a horse, when it stopped, someone in Faîte died. The workaround on that was for them to ride on donkeys. Not quite as quick, but since I could speak to them, they moved along as gracefully as possible, and with little pushback. Bastien hadn't been keen on me riding with Demi, but the only other option was Patrick, since we'd decided to split off into four different groups. Bastien was simply too big to share a donkey with anyone, burly as he was. The idea was that we'd cover more ground and round up more Werewolves if we went in separate directions.

"I hope the others are having better luck than we are. It's been at least an hour, and not a single Werewolf," Bastien griped. "Daisy, if you see any birds around, send them out to look for Weres."

"Will do. I'm guessing this perpetual winter doesn't lend itself to tons of birds, though. I haven't seen a single one this entire time."

"*We should take another way, my queen. Helene is up ahead,*" Demi's donkey warned me.

"Who's Helene?"

Demi stiffened, but replied before the donkey had a chance. "Where did you hear that name?"

"Your donkey said she's up ahead."

Bastien, Demi and Patrick each groaned. "We should go a different way. The Feu Follet won't be all that helpful tonight," Patrick said, bringing his ride to a stop.

"What are you guys talking about?"

Demi slowed his donkey, and his free hand moved to rest atop mine, which was palming his navel. It was a sweet gesture that was subtle enough not to make Bastien any more upset than he already was, but reminded me of the many ways Demi had been gentle with me. "The Feu Follet are little Fae that look like small lights. They flicker through the darkness, illuminating a path to follow. The problem is, it always leads travelers into danger. The trick is that they look so pretty, and they show up when people need a little light to follow. Riders don't question the mercy usually; they just follow wherever it leads, which most of the time is straight into a swift attack."

Bastien added, "Their leader is Helene, but there are thousands of them all over Éireland. I don't feel like dealing with them tonight, guys. We'll go a different way."

I frowned as the guys led the donkeys away from the direction we had been headed. "But wait, if there's danger, couldn't that mean the Werewolves are up ahead? I mean, is that something they might lure us toward?" I checked in with my gut to confirm. "My Compass is telling me that we should keep going in that direction."

Demi mulled over my question. "It's possible you're right. But if Helene is lighting the way, that means whatever's at the end of the lighted path is certainly more harrowing than your average creature. Perhaps a whole pack of them."

My thumb brushed up and down on his stomach. "Well, then what are we waiting for? Isn't this what we've been searching for?"

"Aye," Patrick replied with a gravity to his tone that made me hesitate. "Why again did we leave Cross Shot with another group? Seems like he'd be better used protecting the queen."

I blew a loud raspberry and batted my hand at him. "I'm fine. Not nearly as breakable as everyone thinks I am."

Demi stroked my knuckles with the pad of his thumb. "Nothing will break you if I'm around. Stay close."

Bastien grumbled, but didn't object when everyone turned their donkeys around and headed back down the pathway to doom. The woods felt overly quiet in the wintery wonderland that lit the ground. The moon's reflection danced off the thick blankets of snow. It almost seemed to glitter with iridescence as our donkeys cantered through the drifts that came up to their haunches. I reached my free arm down and patted our ride's hindquarters. "I can't imagine how difficult this would be without you, baby. Thank you for helping."

"Anything for the Voix. When word reached that ye were in Avalon last year, all of us in Éireland were trying to convince our owners to take us to Avalon to meet ye. Some even ran off with their masters on the saddle, screaming the whole way. Tha I get to carry ye on a mission? I'll be the envy of every animal in the forest, tha's for certain."

"Would it help if you told them all that I thought you had a gorgeous chestnut flank? Because you do. Absolutely breathtaking." It was a sweet fib. He was a normal brown donkey, but his back stiffened and his hooves trod with renewed purpose at the compliment.

"I think tha might make its way through the forest. Thanks, my queen."

Demi chuckled, his thumb tucking itself between his

stomach and the inside of my wrist, so he could stroke the tender flesh there discreetly. "Always too gracious for your own good. Still charming every creature you meet, I see. It's nice to know Avalon hasn't changed you all that much."

I reflected on Demi's observation, and decided to draw a modicum of comfort from it. Some days I barely recognized my life, much less myself. To have kindness as my touchstone to which my friends could recognize me felt like a warm hug for my insides. "Thanks, Romeo. That was sweet of you. Sometimes I worry I've changed so much, I won't be able to recognize myself in the mirror anymore. That you can see that parts of me are still rattling around inside unbroken? That helps."

"I could see the goodness in you from continents away. It was your sweetness that drew me to you first, and then second were your lips."

I hid my embarrassed smile in the center of his back. "Hey, now. We can't talk about things like my lips anymore."

I could hear the churlish grin in Demi's tone when he replied with a cheeky, "Can I think about your lips, then?"

I turned my head from side to side against his back. "Not if you want Bastien to be cool. I think I've stretched his patience as far as it'll go at this point."

"It's good for a man to be on his toes every now and then. Let him remember the prize he's stolen from every other man. I would have given anything to be your suitor."

I was about to scold Demi and remind him that we

couldn't indulge in that kind of talk, when a light caught my eyes up ahead. "Oh! Is that them? The Foofy Fillets?"

"It is. The Feu Follet. Hold tight to me," Demi instructed, securing my hand to his toned stomach.

Never in my life did I guess I would have the kind of luck that would give Demi back to me. Though, upon second thought, Demi wasn't mine anymore. It actually made perfect sense that Faîte would give my boyfriend back to me after I was happily settled with my husband.

The lights that beckoned to us were about as tall as an egg, and thin as a permanent marker. When we got closer, I saw that they were tiny human-like people. Little fairies in the Tinkerbell tradition. Their heads tilted back and forth with the wind, making them look like broken-off taper candles that were lit from base to tip. There were dozens lining the way on either side in front of us, letting out a tinkling laughter that made me frown. I didn't much like the idea of my miniature guides laughing at me, drawing glee from my inevitable doom. "Careful, Demi. They're super happy about leading us here."

"How can you tell?"

"Well, the laughter was a big clue."

"What laughter?"

My nose scrunched in confusion. "The little light guys. They're laughing at us. Don't you hear that?"

Demi paused, straining his ear to the side to pick up any new sounds. "Nothing. I wonder if it's your unknown languages ability kicking in. Listen closely for signs that it's Weres we're dealing with, and how many."

I didn't think coming right out and asking would do a whole lot of good, so I played dumb, collecting information I hoped to piece together into something useful. I picked out the words *"yummy," "bait,"* and *"devour,"* so I guessed we were on the right track.

"I can hear them up ahead!" Patrick announced when sounds of animal grunts interrupted the little fairies' excited ramblings.

"Tear their heads off!" I heard one of the Feu Follet chant. *"Then they'll all have missing noggins!"*

I fought the urge to scowl at their bad manners, and kept my ear attuned to anything else that might give a few clues.

"The big one might be able to draw first blood and break the Were's curse, but he'll slice so true, it'll kill them before they can enjoy being cured." I heard little dude clap with glee. *"Either way, someone's going to die!"*

"You guys are total jags!" I scolded them, indignant. "Don't you care that the Weres are hurting people? Is that all we are to you? Entertainment?"

The little lights on either side of the wintry path all paused, and then started jumping up and down with sheer joy. *"It's the* Voix! *The* Voix *has come to Éireland. Shine brighter! Lead her to the Werewolves. This should be a good show."*

I grumbled at the mob mentality they shared. They

seemed like a single brain, flickering the same thought down the row we traveled. Demi's body was stiff with tension as he guided us to what would certainly be a fight, his hand atop mine the entire time. "I can hear the wolves! Let your net down, Patrick. Charge!"

Though Patrick was supposedly the leader of the Dullahan, he followed Demi's directions without hesitation, whipping out a rope net and throwing the end to Demi, who caught the tie without a blink. They each gripped the edge of the net, and drove their donkeys to a gallop into the thicket of trees that grew denser the closer we got.

I heard the wolves before I saw them. I'd been searching for tracks in the snow of pawprints, not remembering until just then that when Lugh and I had met Malone and Nolan, they'd been human on the bottom, and rabid wolf on top.

When the Werewolves came into view, I gasped at the bare human feet that stretched up into a human body, but ended with an overlarge wolf's shoulders and head. The red eyes locked in on us, and as they charged, I closed my lips through a scream.

29

PUTTING ON A GOOD SHOW FOR THE VIEWERS

The dozens of Feu Follet gathered around the clearing to form a sort of ring of death, chanting for either side to shed more blood. It didn't seem like they cared who won, only that there was a fight that ended in a bloody battle. Demi and Patrick had been thoroughly trained by Madigan, and knew exactly what to do. Just before it seemed we might collide with our prey, the donkeys split off in separate directions, but the net lengthened on Patrick's side, permitting enough rope to wrap the seven Werewolves in a tight mishmash of netting they couldn't make sense of. Not only was it dark, but as the donkeys reached the top of the circle they'd traveled, the net tied around the Weres, squeezing them into a group that just shouldn't be. Weres bit and clawed at the net and at each other, trying to break free from the thing that had so easily ensnared them. We were the traveling trap, and I wouldn't have it any other way in a situation like this.

Bastien hopped down when the net was secure enough to contain the wolves. He tightened the ends, throwing a few punches when one of them snapped their fangs in his direction. "Demi, bring Rosie and let's do this!"

Demi dismounted and helped me off the donkey, who warned me not to go near the Weres. I had a hard time finding a spot to touch them where they wouldn't gouge me, but eventually my hand landed on one of their arms. I yanked the sweaty hand through the netting, holding on for two whole seconds before the Were's body went limp, and he fell into the snow. His brethren trampled his now completely furry body as Bastien tightened the net, so no other Werewolves escaped. I made it through four more healings before I was bitten, my hand bleeding on the snow as Bastien punched the offender seconds before I was able to heal him. It was chaos, but we were making progress.

"Are you okay?" Bastien shouted, but I couldn't imagine anything mattering less in this situation. The cured Werewolves were groaning and howling their anguish at the lives they'd been cursed to muddle through, and the mercy that getting yourself back after so much struggle wracked a person with.

As soon as the last Werewolf was cured, I dropped to my knees and threw my body atop the pile of yelping wolves. They were crying out for forgiveness, reliving the woe that brought them to this dreadful place. "It's alright, babies. It's okay. You're all okay now. You don't have to be monsters anymore. You can just be yourselves." I sighed atop them, rubbing my face in their fur just to feel the softness.

I was pulled off the pile in the next breath, and Bastien bandaged my hand with trembling fingers that were stiff from the cold. "That's enough playing with monsters for you."

I smirked up at him, my expression stiff and tired. "If only. This is just round one. Here's hoping they all go this smoothly."

Bastien frowned at my hand, bringing it up to show me the bandage. "You call this smooth?"

"I call this success." My eyes danced with triumph as part one of the plan finally left the station with banners waving high. "We're doing it. We're actually doing it!"

"Let's get back to the bunker. That's enough for tonight."

I shook my head and bent down to scoop up one of the mocking assjack Feu Follets. She glowed in my palm, clapping at the show that had given her some good old-fashioned bloodshed. "What's your name?"

"Helene," she replied, her thin lips curved up in a smile. Her eyes danced with mischief, and she started to do an obnoxious dance with plenty of hip gyrations. She was clothed only in light, which blurred out her PG-13 bits, but not by much. "We're all named Helene. You're bleeding!" she pointed out with glee.

"I am. You want to see more? You want an all-nighter filled with nothing but harrowing stakes and possible gore?"

Helene jumped up and down, her miniature bosom bouncing with delight. "Yes! We want more! Give us more! I want to see this one in action. The way he punched the Werewolves in the face? I've never seen someone that wild. Mostly they just scream and run, but he fought back!"

"Good. This is Bastien, and if you can take us to more Werewolves right now, he'll do it all over again. As many times as you can take us to one of these packs, he'll put on a good show for you."

"Oh, goody!" She hopped from my hand onto Bastien's shoulder, tracing her finger on his earlobe and stroking the back of her wrist down his neck to give him the shivers. "Follow me, big boy," she offered in a sultry voice. Well, as sultry as a smurf's voice could get, I guess.

Bastien quirked an eyebrow at me. "You really think this is a good idea? You're bleeding."

"So? I think this is the perfect time to get as many healings done as we can. Don't you want to go home?"

Bastien ignored the pixie on his shoulder and leaned in to kiss me. "I want that more than anything. You do, too? You want our old life back?"

I let out a nervous laugh as the wolves started slipping

out of the net and stretching out their limbs. "There's nothing I want more. Let's get this over with."

Bastien's grin was a sight that was more uplifting to my soul than anything else on the planet. His crooked grin leaped onto my face, kissing me without concern for who was watching. As the snow fell around, the world slowed so that it was just us – only and ever us.

30

WEREWOLF VERSUS VAMPIRE

"I've been waiting for a big man like you to come around. Take off your shirt for us, Bastien."

I giggled at the bawdy things Helene was catcalling into Bastien's ear. The guys all concurred that the Feu Follets just sounded like high-pitched unintelligible murmurings. Only I could pick out the words. They gave me so many good laughs as I listened to Helene call him "big man," "hunky sailor," and "walking eye candy." I wasn't about to argue with the girl; she was dead on.

The lights fluttered ahead, leading us to a small town where the houses were unlit on the inside, and looked shut tight out of fear. I caught a few faces peering out into the night, eyes darting this way and that to suss out from which way the danger might come.

Helene, the little light sneak, didn't mention that we

were walking into an ambush. We didn't have time to cast out the net, but had to resort to drawing swords to get them off of us. There were easily twenty Werewolves, and they jumped out at us from the woods that surrounded the terrified villagers. It was a town held hostage, and we were the cavalry on donkeys.

"Hold on, Rosie!" Demi cried when our ride bucked. A Werewolf sank his teeth deep into the rump of our donkey, causing him to buck and thrash in the fray.

It had seemed like such a solid plan at the time, trusting the Feu Follet to lead us into the danger we sought out. I didn't put it together that we wouldn't have the upper hand we desperately needed in each doomed situation we were taken to.

"It's alright. Calm down, honey!" I tried to call out to the donkey, but it was no use. Vicious claws ripped me from my perch, tearing me from Demi and throwing me to the ground. My hand on his cured him, but it was too late. Too many wolfmen pounced atop me, tearing at my arms and legs as I flailed in the madness.

I landed punches as hard as I could, and gripped onto hairy limbs with all my might, keeping my mind on curing as I tried to escape. I knew healing them was my only route to escape, so I focused on that as much as I could. The pain could wait until later. Later, I would feel it all, let it wash over me and debilitate every movement. For now, it was cure or be killed.

One by one, the wolfmen lost their carnivorous

momentum, collapsing in an exhausted gust once the cure ran through them. Bastien, Patrick and Demi did their best to extract me, but there were just too many wolves to call it a fair fight. The only chance we had was to heal them, which diminished their numbers.

I screamed when Patrick ran one of the Weres through, stabbing him through the side and spilling his blood all over the pure white of the snow. I knew that if I didn't heal them all quickly, more would suffer the same fate. I contemplated freezing them, but knew I didn't have a solid enough handle on climate control to be able to pull that off without possibly harming them for real.

I stumbled to my feet, breathing through my teeth to try and make it past the pain I promised I would give myself plenty of freedom to feel later.

"Here, Rosie!" Bastien called. He had a Weredude pinned in a wrestling hold that might not last as long as it would take me to get over there.

I limped through the snow, racing my way to Bastien as the other Weres began to circle me, cutting me off from help. Demi and Patrick had their net ready, but now I was in the center of the fray, so I would be smooshed in with the beasts if the net closed in on them. It was all I could do to think through the fear that clawed at my insides, and the searing pain that dripped down my legs and arms.

It was when one of the Weres growled at me, and his fangs caught the glimmer of the moonlight that it dawned on me how much of a threat I could be. I wasn't willing to fight with knives, but I had weapons of my own I could access that would hurt without killing, if I was careful.

Instead of waiting for them to pounce, I made the first move, focusing all my football-pounding aggression on the Werewolf directly in front of me. I charged toward him without holding myself back for once.

I wouldn't be the weak one. I wouldn't be the liability. Deep down, I knew that when the people I loved were in danger, I had a well of untapped violence I could channel. Avalon had been wrong about me. I wasn't the princess. I wasn't fit for a crown or the lavish things in life that came with perfect posture and on-cue smiles. I was a savage girl, and in moments like these, I relished every bit of my dual nature.

The Werewolf saw my chase and bent his knees to charge at me in return. I didn't shy away from the collision, but welcomed it. The Were's jaws snapped at me, but mine were quicker. I bearhugged the dude, and sank my fangs down into the meat of his shoulder, slicing through the furry skin until I struck oil.

Demi cried out, and Bastien let out a roar of distress, but I was in the zone. By the time the first flood of acrid blood hit my tongue, the wolfman's body had mutated in to all wolf, leaving his mind all human. I don't know how he found the wherewithal to put himself smack into battle-mode on the other side than he'd been fighting on previously, but he quickly rolled on top of me, shielding me with his furry body as the others pounced.

Over and over again, I bit and drained, taking in blood I didn't want, so that it would weaken them just enough for me to get a good grip to take them down. By the time the last few around me fell, I wasn't sure whose blood I was wearing more of – theirs or mine. I was trembling from my own blood loss, but I knew nothing vital was gushing.

The others were struggling with their few leftover Weres, so I tried to crawl to my feet to help out. I didn't see the villagers who'd come out of their huts. I didn't hear their cries of fear, or make out that they were shouting, "Vampire!" as much as they were clamoring for the removal of the Werewolves.

I didn't see the wadded-up sock that was stuffed in my mouth, nor the black sack until it was shoved over my head, and I was hoisted over the back of a horse. A man I didn't know shoved my head down, so my butt stuck up in the air. My hands were quickly tied behind my back, and off the horse went, galloping in to the night.

31

ANOTHER VAMPIRE, DEAD BY MORNING

I tried to tell the horse I was on to knock it off, that I didn't want to be taken from Bastien. The sock in my mouth made communication impossible, though I heard the horse's fears clear as day. *"Vampire. Vampire. To the bunker. Another Vampire, dead by morning."*

I gulped and tried to scream for Cailleach or Kerdik, but I couldn't touch my ring to my heart to properly summon them. I wanted to escape, to fight my way free, but I was so awkwardly tied to the horse, I couldn't gain any momentum in my movements. When we leapt over barriers, I was Heimliched, and nearly vomited into the used sock. The man on the steed patted my butt in a "there, there" kind of way, which made me want to kick him through my boiling rage.

We rode for what seemed like hours, the blood rushing to my head and making me pass out a few times along the way. Each time I would rouse, it was with renewed fight that somehow, someway, I would get out of this mess. That determination lasted until unconsciousness claimed me again. It wasn't all that effective of an escape plan.

I awoke to hands on me, taking me down from the horse with care not for my body, but for their own. I was led in a headlock over uneven terrain, my shoes tripping over rocks and roots that were buried deep. I finally decided not to make the trek any easier for the jags who thought abducting me would be a swell idea, and let my body go limp, saving my energy for an escape I had yet to figure out.

"This one's barely alive! I thought we were going to burn them all on Sundays."

"I didn't hurt her none. She was biting Werewolves. Tha's why she's so banged up."

"No, she didn't. Tha's mad, tha is. Was she tha rabid?"

"I guess so. Saw it with my own two eyes. She was tearing out the throats of Werewolves, going through a dozen in a couple of minutes, and salivating for more."

I wanted to argue, but the sock made conversation problematic. I hadn't torn out anyone's throat, and the wolf blood was disgusting – a means to an end. I'd helped save that jackhole's village, but sure, I'm the danger. I'm the monster. That made perfect sense.

"This one? She's just a tiny thing. Up ye get, wee Vamp." Dude hefted me into his arms, carrying me like a baby through the snow. I took a few minutes to catch my breath, taking inventory of my limbs to make sure they were all fully functional. I hoped I hadn't lost so much blood that I would be useless once I got my bearings about me. "Open the door. Tell Finnegan we've got a wee one for the pyre."

I gulped at the chuckle as someone mussed my hair through the black sack. I wanted to growl at the men who took me where I didn't want to go, but guessed that wouldn't win me a whole lot of popularity points. I needed to make it out alive, and didn't have the first clue how to manage that.

I was carried through several rooms where people thought it was a great idea to pat me on the head and chuckle, as if they knew something devious that I didn't. Several of them spat at me, while a few knocked me upside the head without warning, cursing me as I was carried off.

"Tha's enough, now," the dude who carried me scolded someone who hit me too hard. "Finnegan wants them burned, not beaten. We ain't savages."

I didn't know the man who carried me, but I clung to him for no reason other than that he'd almost said something kind of nice. Not actually nice, mind you, but I would take what I could get in this place. I tried to spit out the sock yet again, but it was wedged between my teeth so tightly that my jaw ached, and felt winched painfully wide.

I heard the clanging of iron, and too many people wailing their pain. Several of them made a case for why they should be let go to the man who brought me in with them, but I could tell it was falling on deaf ears. None of their stories mattered to this vigilante group. They wanted the Vampires killed so their land could return to normal. Anything contrary to that wasn't a selling point they were willing to buy into. We were the savages. We were the danger. But now we were the caged.

I tried not to sob too loudly when I was set down on a concrete floor, but the bang that echoed through my already bruised and bloody body gave the dude the satisfaction I hadn't wanted to give up so easily.

The black sack was removed from my head, but the sock remained in place, and my hands were still secured behind my back. The man knelt down in front of me as I blinked my new world into focus. There were rows and rows of tiny cells like the one I was held in. The basement was windowless, and stank of urine and despair. There was barely enough room for most of the prisoners to stand – the taller ones hunching over to compensate. They could move their elbows out to the sides, but that was it. We were chickens stuffed into a coop, with a farmer who didn't care if we made it out alive. We were destined for the slaughterhouse, so our comfort was of no consideration. Dozens and dozens of cells stretched down the row across from where I sat, each one filled with a vengeful or tearful Vampire who looked like they were all without a solid prayer to get them through.

The man who'd carried me in had red hair, freckles, and the body of a lumberjack who'd given up chopping trees so he could kidnap Vampires and take them here. He didn't look mean, instead his expression was resigned. "Hello, wee monster. I'm Rudy, one of the guards down here. Do ye know why you've been brought in?"

I shook my head, though I knew exactly why.

"When Master Kerdik accidentally let the lost magic slip out into Faîte, some of ye were infected with the Vampire curse. It's our job to purge Éireland of the darkness, so our children have a safe place to play. Ye can understand tha, aye?"

I made to answer him, but it came out all muffled.

Rudy gave me a sad smile and shook his head. "Ye can make your case all ye want, but this place is heated with the bodies of Vampires. It gives warmth to the people who give hope back to Éireland. Tha gets to be your gift to the motherland. No matter what ye say, tha's how it's going to go. One by one, you're carried out and ye don't come back, but by the ashes in the sky. Understand?"

Images of horrific deaths of who knows how many people that had been burned alive flooded through my brain. Unbidden, I saw myself flailing in a giant woodburning stove, my flesh melting off of me, and the woodsmen roasting marshmallows over my bones. I let out a bleat of fright, but that was all I would allow him to have. He didn't seem particularly vindictive, only that he was resigned to this being the only way.

"I'll take your gag out, and you'll stay here until it's time for ye to serve Éireland." He shook his head at my complexion. "Jays, they went a little heavy-handed with ye. They shouldn't have done tha. We don't torture the Vamps here. Just end them as humanely as we can. I'll have a chat with Finnegan."

I knew I probably looked terrible. I'd been crying, so my face was streaked with blood. The second the sock was pried from my lips, I gusted out, "Untouchable!"

"What?"

"I'm married to Bastien the Bold. Look at my mark! I'm Untouchable, no matter if I'm Vampire or not."

Rudy frowned at me, angling his head to get a better look at my neck. "Well, something's there, but it's burned. What did they do to ye?"

"The tattoo's on my wrist, too. I need to speak with Finnegan, or whoever's in charge. I'm the Avalon Rose, and if you burn me like this, it's going to cause a war between Avalon and Éireland!"

Rudy's eyes went wide as he gasped. He stumbled back, falling on his butt in shock. "Now tha's a plea I haven't heard before. Ye say you're the Avalon Rose? Ye know it's high treason to pretend to be royalty if ye aren't."

I contemplated asking them to bring an animal here for me to speak to, but I worried the doom and gloom nature of this place might spook any furry little friend into inaction out of fear. "Get Duke Lot out here to verify it's me. I promise I'll sit and wait patiently, but you have to contact them. If Lot comes here and says I'm not the

Avalon Rose, you can roast a whole pig over my body, and I won't fight you on it."

Rudy inched out of the cage and shoved it closed with his boot. The latch clicked into place, and my heart sank. It wasn't until he stood and brushed off his pants that I heard him mutter, "I'll talk to Finnegan, and see what he says about ye. If you're lying to me, you'll be next in line for the furnace, wee Vamp."

His boots were heavy on the concrete as he walked out of the dungeon I'd been sequestered to. The lantern was taken off the hook on his way out, and when the solid door shut, the faces of the anguished Vampires around me faded to black, plunging everyone into a mess of terrified darkness.

Love the book? Leave a review.

32

DANGEROUS GIRL

*H*ere's a free preview of *Dangerous Girl*, Book II in the *Faîte Falling* series.

BEING ALONE WITH YOUR THOUGHTS IS A THING MOST PEOPLE pay good money for during yoga classes or meditation retreats. I didn't have to spend a dime on the dungeon I'd been thrown in, thanks to the fangs I hadn't asked for. When the lost magic escaped into Faîte, it infected some people with a Vampire curse, and others with a Werewolf curse. I learned that if I touched the Werewolves or the *Farouche* Vampires, I could cure them, sucking the poison back to where it came from, inside my ring.

I was an *Attelage* Vampire, though, and because Uncle Dub was thorough, I couldn't cure myself or my kind. I'd used my fangs to weaken the Werewolves I'd been fighting, in an attempt to get close enough to cure them. It had worked, but when the villagers saw me chomp down and drink the blood, my "thank you for saving our village" card must've gotten lost in the mail. I was swiftly kidnapped and taken to this stinking bunker, where the vigilantes of Éireland were desperately trying to free their land of the higher magic that had seized them so abruptly.

It was a solid plan, except that *Attelage* Vampires like myself didn't usually feed off random victims, like the *Farouche* Vampires did. Those dudes had gone rabid, and fed on their victims until the last drop of blood was drained. *Attelage* Vamps only fed on the blood of the person they'd had their first drink from. We had rational thought, and were still pretty much ourselves, while the *Farouche* were rabid and didn't have language. Bastien was my mate, and we'd made our peace with the situation nearly two years ago when it all hit the fan.

The rest of the world? Not so much. My father disowned me, and turned me out of the kingdom I'd restored to him. Now Duke Lot was in charge of District 1, so that I could live a peaceful life in Common – the earth we all know and love. Ice cream. Indoor plumbing. Fast food. Grad school. All the things I needed and missed, and had given up to be back here in Faîte, sucking the lost magic out of the land as best I could.

I didn't expect to be abducted, or that people were still so set in their ways that they couldn't evaluate the situation and see that *Attelage* Vamps weren't a danger to the public.

It didn't matter, though. People love being right more than they love justice, I'd learned. Now I was on the docket to be burned so they didn't have to reevaluate what they were doing.

That was how I landed myself in the dungeon of gnashing teeth and endless tears. Around every six hours or so, two burly men would come in and yank a Vampire out of their cell, taking them to the furnace, where they were burned alive. Their bodies heated the bunker, which was supposed to be their way of being useful to society, since apparently once we were infected, we had no purpose in Faîte anymore.

Three Vampires had been taken from the dark dungeon and escorted to the furnace while I waited in hopes that Rudy – the dude who'd carried me inside – would tell the up-and-ups that there was an Untouchable in their dungeon. That shouldn't really be happening, under the highest law of the land. It was supposed to be my Get Out of Jail Free card, yet here I sat, encased behind iron bars as I waited out my doom. This time he'd left us with a lantern. I'd thought it was a mercy to keep us from the dark, but I quickly learned the dim light only amped up the fear. The concrete walls of the windowless base-ment dungeon we were kept in was one long rectangle, with dozens of cells running down both walls. It was cold here, despite our fellow citizens' bodies being burned to warm the place. The whole place stank of urine and terror.

I wasn't sure which was worse as both stenches seemed to seep into my pores.

I sat with my legs crossed, trying to will calm into my soul by my body setting the precedent. Other than the fact that my arms were still tied behind my back, I looked the picture of poise, ready for the cover of any yoga magazine. Well, I was bloody and bruised from the fight with the Werewolves, but other than that, totally Zen.

Start Book II in the *Faîte Falling* series,
and read *Dangerous Girl* today!

ABOUT THE AUTHOR

USA Today bestselling author Mary E. Twomey lives in Michigan with her three adorable children. She enjoys reading, writing, vegetarian cooking, and telling her children fantastic stories about wombats.

While she loves writing fantasy, dystopian, and paranormal tales for her readers, Mary also writes romance under the name Tuesday Embers, and cozy mysteries under the name Molly Maple.

Visit her online at www.maryetwomey.com, and sign up for her newsletter, so you never miss a new release.